The Strange Case of Mademoiselle P.

ALSO BY BRIAN O'DOHERTY

Inside the White Cube
Object and Idea
American Masters: the Voice and the Myth

Pantheon Books · New York

The
Strange Case
of
Mademoiselle
P.

A NOVEL

Brian O'Doherty

All rights reserved under International and Pan-American
Copyright Conventions. Published in the United States by
Pantheon Books, a division of Random House, Inc., New
York, and simultaneously in Canada by Random House of
Canada Limited, Toronto.

Grateful acknowledgment is made to Macdonald & Co. Ltd.
for permission to freely adapt from *Mesmerism* by Doctor
Mesmer, edited with an Introductory Monograph by Gilbert
Frankau. Adaptation is based on the 1948 English translation
of Mesmer's *Memoire sur la decouverte du
Magnetisme Animal*.

Library of Congress Cataloging-in-Publication Data

O'Doherty, Brian.
The strange case of Mademoiselle P. :
a novel/Brian O'Doherty.
p.   cm.
ISBN 0-679-41208-5
1. Mesmer, Franz Anton, 1734–1815—Fiction. 2. Paradies.
Maria Theresa von, 1770–1824—Fiction. 3. Austria—
History—Maria Theresa, 1740–1780—Fiction. I. Title.
PS3565.D46S77   1992
813'.54—dc20   91-50750

Book Design by M. Kristen Bearse

Manufactured in the United States of America
35798642

For Barbara Novak

The Strange Case of Mademoiselle P.

—— · *1* · ——

*S*he said nothing, but drifted towards me. Her mother, who had arranged this meeting, was voluble, dividing her discourse between respectful address to me and sharp cautions to her daughter. I seated the girl by the high window and looked into her eyes. Their suppuration had left fresh trails on either side of her nose which, from previous rivulets drying, had the sheen of snails' tracks. Indeed it seemed to me that her eyes had been replaced by two vigorous snails. They rolled and bulged in a way totally at variance with the features around them. The face was patient, though at this time a little anxious in expression. When I removed her hat, I saw that her hair had been cut short, not in any fashionable way, nor in preparation for a wig, but as casually as if it had been grass. Above the temples it was patchy, almost bald.

"Sir," said the mother, hurrying forward, "for two months we encased her head in plaster. For what purpose? On the best advice, sir. To hold her head still, to give the eyes peace, to prevent her twitching around like a marionette. Leeches, blisters, purgatives, everything according to the doctors. And the shocks, shocks to the eyeballs, sir. A hundred at a time, thousands, thousands, each painful as a knife—"

At this point the mother reached out and began to stagger with the violence of her discourse. My servant François placed her in a chair, where she started to weep inordinately and babble in a way that seemed to me to have much precedent.

"Oh my child, my beautiful child—cursed

by God—three years of brightness—fifteen years of darkness—what have we done to deserve such torment—our only child—who would marry her with such an affliction—help us, help us—if God is in his heaven, remove this curse—my child, my child, eternal darkness, darkness, torments—my innocent chi——"

Her words began to trail off into a long *i* sound, succeeded by a long *o*, this being succeeded in turn by a long *e*. This extended wailing sounded quite eerie and unpleasant. She was now sobbing in an exaggerated fashion while grasping François's hand, pressing it between her breasts and burying her face in his sleeve, which he lent her with some discomfort. On turning my gaze back to the girl, I was astonished at the change in her. Her eyes were now without pupils. Only the whites showed. Her mouth was turned upside down by the action of her platysmas, which in their contraction had aged and furrowed her neck. With her eyes rolling upward so intensely, I had the fancy she was trying to see inside of her skull. I had my first inkling that it would be necessary to separate the child from the mother.

My attempts to gain a history of the girl's

affliction from her mother were partly successful. When I had met her father the previous day, he had offered some essential
details. He appeared to me to be one of those
careful men one finds around court, who while
watching the weather vane maintains a distance which passes for dignity and is often mis-
taken for wisdom. He had an exact date for
the onset of her affliction—9th December '62.
I was seeing the girl now, fifteen years later,
on January 20th. I knew something of her already. She was well thought of at court, and
her accomplishments would have honored a
fully healthy woman.

In every case there are problems. Nothing
is clear-cut or simple, and we practice our art
in an arena very different from that which history reads back upon us, or which we read
back upon the past. History sees things simply,
instructed by the results; success or failure is
history's criterion. I was aware that the gains
I had made with Franzl could easily be thrown
away. The case was similar. But this girl's circle both offered opportunity and gave me
pause. I knew that the Empress had taken an
interest in her through, I imagine, her father's
offices. She had often played for the Empress.
The Empress, I knew, had placed her under

the care of her chief physician, Stoerk, whom I held in affection as examiner for my degree, and who had honored me as a witness at my wedding. I hadn't seen much of Stoerk in recent years. I knew, however, that his attempt to alleviate the girl's symptoms had not been successful. Indeed her father's request to place her under my care was probably a last resort, based on the rumors of Franzl's cure. I say rumors because it has been my distressful fate that each of my cures has been followed by a shadow, the shadow of disbelief. What I do is fragile. The mind itself is a shadow that inhabits our substance in elusive and contradictory ways. Like the tides, the shadow lengthens and shrinks with the universal fluid. In that fluid many forces slide one into the other, like a telescope that reaches from the intimate eye of the observer to the distant stars, the celestial harmonies which we, in our brief circulation through this world, echo and embody. We are both substance and shadow, and it is the shadow that moves our substance through the magnetic force. This is hard for men to understand, particularly medical men, who believe that the substance is primary. I had no wish to cure the girl and inflame Stoerk, old friend and mentor that he was.

I told the mother what I had told the father the previous day. That if the body was dead, the spirit could not function; but that if the body lived, the spirit sometimes fell into a swoon, a darkness. To call into that darkness, to listen for its echo, was sometimes possible. To awaken the spirit, to coax it back to occupy its body, was a slow and hazardous procedure. To that end, I would examine the girl's eyes; if their body was dead, there was nothing to be done. But if the organs themselves were without fault, the darkness could be lifted from them.

Yesterday the father listened without listening, as indeed the mother did today. They wished for reassurance, not explanations. To them, I was speaking magic, or sorcery. I expected more from the father, who was an educated man, though I did not know of what his secretarial duties at court consisted. It has always been my belief that it is to the doctor's advantage if the patient—and in the case of young patients, their families—understand the nature of the treatment, although I should remind myself that some are incapable of this understanding. When I speak to them of "animal spirits," some think I speak of dogs and cats. If I had my way—which of course I shall not—I would have every student read Wolff's *Rational Thoughts on the Functions of the Parts of Men, Animals and Plants*. It is in good honest German and available to all. Behind him, of course, stands the great Descartes, whose reason is a light to which all living things turn. Perhaps this is where my insistence on the education of the patient originates. There is no mystery that should escape precision of thought or the light of reason. I do not go as far as my beloved Wolff—that God can be transformed into an equation—but if science deserves the name, it must be conducted in the light of reason in the classic manner. First the data, then the hypothesis, then the proof. Without this habit of mind, we are merely spinning like a compass in a cluster of magnets.

The girl's eyes were in a dreadful state—twitching, blinking, suppurating with a yellow pus, and rolling wildly whenever I spoke to her. With her partial baldness from the wretched plaster, and the marks of leeches and bleedings on her arms, she was a woebegone sight. Her general condition gave me pause. Here was a living result of the art of medicine as practiced by my colleagues. How much better she would have been with no treatment at all. Too often one sees the dolorous results of medical intervention, the accumulated insults it delivers to body and mind in the name of theories that ignore the mind, that are unacquainted with the harmonies between mind, body, and the planets. How often have I had to defend the thesis for my degree on "The Influence of the Planets on the Human Body." As I looked at these orbs, clouded with disease, pain, and dark to the world, how could my thoughts not move out to the heavenly spheres which in their harmonies can bring all living things to light, including the organs through which light enters the soul? I examined the eyes carefully. The pupils responded to light. The eyes were alive, but separated from the light by a darkness of the mind.

My first condition was that the girl—or Marie Thérèse as I now called her (she was named, I imagine, after the Empress in a courtier's gesture)—should live in my clinic, away from the everyday influence of her mother. How much her parents had contributed to her condition, I did not know. But to coax the light back into her eyes I needed her full attention. After much discussion among themselves, the parents agreed to my terms. I subsequently tried to extract from the mother details of that occasion when the darkness had descended on her daughter. Why a three-year-old child should suddenly become blind was mysterious, and mysterious to the mother, who assigned the responsibility to a Godly whim. Did some awful sight present itself that left her mind no option but to eclipse it? How did the invisible fluids that ebb and flow within each of our bodies withdraw, leaving her eyes high and dry? But why her? Why were not a whole group of children blinded on that date if the animating fluid withdrew? These are large questions. Not only did Marie Thérèse present me with a case fascinating in itself, but she became the vehicle of my thinking on disease and its origins.

Though Marie Thérèse could not see what lay around her, my quarters are designed to set the mind at rest, to reduce the extraneous distractions that jar the senses unevenly in the world outside. Carpets, curtains, and the low melodious voices of my assistants and servants further this intention. Frequently I hired musicians to play, usually strings and a flute from among the friends of young Wolfgang, whose father I hold in much affection. The girl's response did not surprise me. Particularly when young Wolfgang tested the new spinet, her trembling ceased, her eyes no longer twitched into grotesque extremes, and the high flush on her neck and forehead died away to her cheeks. I always spoke to her in a calm and steady voice, modulating each sentence to prepare it for entry into her mind. During my treatments, I recline the patient in a large easy chair, which gives me access to every part of the body with minimum shiftings. Our excessive fashions often hinder the movement of my hands, especially with women, whose dresses, skirts, pads, hoops, and other paraphernalia are absurd. While they make a fine show on a Sunday promenade, they have little virtue in my premises.

The girl Marie Thérèse, as all of us quickly noted, was a person of extraordinary sweetness. I formed the opinion that outside the orbit of her parents she flourished like a spring flower. She was, as expected, somewhat passive, but that passivity, it seemed to me, was a result of a highly developed patience. If something was not pleasant—and here I include her mother's daily visits—she wore a pleasing smile while she ever so slightly nodded her head and upper body in a faint but regular rhythm. She was both present and far away at such times, or gave that impression. She would respond when included in the conversation. She would cover her eyes with her lids, beneath which, as I observed on one occasion when I stole up close to her, her pupils were extremely restless, darting hither and thither while she maintained that ghost of a smile. Her intelligence—always my ally in such cases—manifested itself in every aspect of her conversation, which flowed easily except when I discussed her family life or her illness. The rhythmic nodding of her body then became more exaggerated and rapid, and the smile became an anguished grin, like the tragic mask in the theater.

Since observation is the first rule, I watched her carefully at all times and did not neglect to keep an account of her. To watch a young woman without sight provides equal pleasure and discomfort. There is the pleasure of studying a remarkable young creature as she learns, navigating my rooms hesitantly at first, then with greater confidence, until eventually her movements were so sure that her hand always alighted in the close vicinity of her objective, forcing from me an involuntary nod. Gradually her movements developed that floating quality I had first noticed. My discomfort arose from an unworthy sense of superiority which my sight afforded me. We do, it seems to me, instinctively rank those we meet according to their beauty, and this extends further to imperfections and abnormalities, creating a scale like that at court, where degrees of birth ordain the behavior of those above and below one's station. While this feeling of superiority is not acceptable to reasonable men, I suspect it comes from deep within, and has something animal about it. I have seen animals reject their own imperfect kind. Nature, it seems, has this cruelty, this other form of blindness. All the more reason, then, to transcend our lower natures and place ourselves in proper harmony.

There were occasions, however, when *her* superiority was clear. She occupied herself during the long days with lacemaking, and her hands showed an ingenuity and cunning as if they had their own intelligence. The doilies and laces were of sufficient quality to excite my wife's admiration. My wife, who is easily pleased in most things, admires only those laces which exhibit the highest skills. How Marie Thérèse follows the pattern and develops such intricacies is a mystery to me. The thought raised itself in my mind that at such moments her sight returned without her conscious knowledge. So I discreetly asked her to wear a light blindfold, which she did amiably, but it in no way impaired her skills.

Extraordinary though her lacemaking and knitting were, they seemed trivial when one heard her play the spinet. From the same knowledgeable hands issued a whole range of feelings in bursts, chords and intricacies that reminded me in sound of her skills with the lace. Since I believe deeply in the effect of music on the spirit, this opening, indeed vista, into her inner life when she played, moved me as much as if I were hearing a master piano player. I found myself making adjustments and calculations so that I could come to a proper estimate of her playing. Was I over-affected by her blindness? Did my role as her doctor prejudice me unduly in her favor? Were her selections so much to my taste that my discrimination was disarmed? Looking at her face as she played, sometimes closing my eyes and sharing her darkness (for music sometimes makes us desire a kind of blindness, a place to rest the eyes while the spirit is ravished), I was amazed at the confidence and energy of her attack, and her delicacy and precision, particularly in difficult right-hand passages. She rarely fingered a wrong note.

When one first hears any pianist, one's ears

hold to an almost automatic schedule; first, does the player reach a level of technical competence that advances player and listener to the next phase of attention—the spirit of the music? After that, I listen for the individuality of the interpretation, the way in which that spirit is recognized, altered, given a reading, as I call it, with its own particular voice. Has the performer entered inside the music to fill it out from within? Or is the spirit of the music assembled, no matter how skillfully from the outside, offering a simulacrum that may be perfectly shaped? These are no easy matters to decipher. Many performers favor a kind of technical perfection, choosing to stay outside the music for the purpose of shaping its line and volume as a cutter shapes a diamond. I favored this practice in my youth, but now find it fits well into my ear but leaves my feelings unaltered. The other fashion at the moment is equally distressing to me—giving to the music more than is in it. This approach exaggerates the musical contours to a kind of fever chart, hurrying along at a slightly faster tempo than the composer intended. This pleases more people than the former practice, but it does not please those of us who aspire to the highest art. Of these, there are never too many. In

talking this over with my musicians, they are
of much the same opinions. I call them "mine"
because they play occasionally for my clinic;
they and Marie Thérèse converse easily, and
she looks forward to their visits.

Marie Thérèse's playing, to my ear, discerns
the spirit of the music well and inflects it cun-
ningly with her own nature. She has the confidence to give a familiar composition a new
edge by fingering slightly off the tempo in
some notes, so that the ear is kept alert in a
familiar piece. She thereby commands a kind
of double attention. One is borne along with
the music, but at the same time the ear is
aware of being asked a question and searches
for the answer. Sometimes the piece ends and
one has not found it, but this leaves one with
a pleasant dissatisfaction. None of this is immediately obvious. The range of her emotions,
the yearning and wit that give her playing
depth and character, waft up from the music,
so that one is slowly cajoled into attention. I
have watched this happen to the courtiers at
a fine concert. Usually their attention is a mask
for wandering thoughts, or so it seems to me,
since simulating attention is their main trade.
But they do have a fine ear for the exceptional.
That much was obvious when I heard her play

at court before she was brought to me—although her affliction may underline her playing to provoke wonder, much as the skills of jugglers and acrobats are appreciated, or worse, those of performing animals, the wonder being that they can do it at all. In addition, the courtiers know that the Empress she is named after has taken a special interest in her, much to her father's delight. Her father leads her to the piano, places her hands upon the keyboard, and, while she gently tests some notes to find her place, stands behind her with his hands on her shoulders until the Empress nods, although on this occasion she nodded with her fan. He makes some signal or pressure on her shoulders and she begins while he tiptoes away.

The young Wolfgang, who pulls droll faces when he finds something of little merit, has watched her—I watched him—with a half-smile and a slightly open mouth, as if drinking in her performance. Wolfgang comes often enough to play for me that he and Marie Thérèse have become, if not friends, warm acquaintances, and I often see him sit beside her, testing a passage on the spinet as they animatedly discuss some point. She has, I think, a growing affection for him, for he pays not the slightest attention to her affliction, and treats her as he would any young girl of talent and pleasing appearance.

Her appearance when she plays is different from what I would have expected. She closes her eyes, yielding herself to a double darkness. But there is no somnambulistic reverie about her face or posture. Her features become expressive, mobile, indeed frequently distorted as if the emotions required the exercise of her features, particularly her mouth. She frowns, she grimaces, she squeezes her eyes tightly, and eyes and mouth are not always symmetrically used. The mouth purses, pouts, stretches, both lips disappear between her teeth, at times she seems in pain or about to weep. As the performance calls for vigor and activity, her facial mime seems not to reflect the music but to drive it on—a kind of playing with her face as much as with her hands. Watching this, one feels her privacy transgressed. But with time, the sideshow of her face becomes an emblem of her deep involvement, which one eventually shares without embarrassment. There is nothing maidenly about her playing. When her attack sends her hands flying over the keys—her fingers flickering like white sticks under the candles—one sees someone at work rather than someone at play. When she stops, hands in lap and face masked by that calm blankness and half-smile, she is again a maidenly creature, demure and tractable as she curtseys to the applause in the direction of the Empress, towards whom her father, now behind her, carefully directs her.

She works constantly at her repertoire, perfecting and adding to it. Her memory is so well trained, and her desire to excel so intense, that her responsibilities to her talent, indeed her profession, augur well for my treatment. There is much that is hidden about her. She has learned well the conventions through which young ladies present themselves. Though modest in nature, she is not innocent of how to cultivate a feminine presence with those hoops and bodices that rustle so fetchingly for some of the male sex. She is never coquettish or trivial. Indeed her mature façade frequently breaks down to reveal a child simulating maturity. Having set her eyes to rest, having limited her mother's visits to one a day, and the father's to twice a week, and having satisfied myself that her affliction was an impediment of the spirit and not of the body, I began my treatments. I decided not to use magnets.

—————— · **2** · ——————

Often when stroking her thighs, I thought it wise to have my wife as witness. To move the fluids in the proper polar directions, it is necessary to mould the body, to follow its contours as one guides the fluids within by the magnetized hands alone. Since no part of the body can declare itself exempt from this process, these movements could, to the common eye, be misinterpreted. The detail is always more obvious than its guiding principle. So when treating young girls especially, it is prudent for my wife—certainly in the beginning—to certify its legitimacy by her presence. With some grandes dames, the misinterpretation is undertaken by themselves, leading to embarrassment for all parties. The crisis is, in most cases, intrinsic to the cure. But the forms that this crisis takes have frequently made it necessary to hire strong assistants who will bear the subject away to a protected room where the crisis can exercise itself fully without distracting other patients. On one occasion I found an assistant taking advantage of this isolation in a way that can be easily imagined, and his departure was followed by rumors that accused me and my assistants of the very transgression for which he had been dismissed. To men of intelligence and insight, such accusations must ring hollow, but life teaches one that these are always in a minority, and one is inevitably led to lower one's opinion of mankind the more one knows of the world—and perhaps of oneself.

My treatment of Marie Thérèse, I was determined, would give rise to no such foolishness. I laid her down on the chaise each morning and afternoon, and with my magnetized gestures and strokings moved the fluid towards head and feet, never urging it impatiently, but sensing as best I could the response of the fluid to my hands as it lay under her skin. It is the insides of the arms and thighs, the flanks, and the neck, and, to some extent, on either side the row of tiny knuckles of the spine that are particularly sensitive to the movement of the fluid. This stroking can, if one is skillful, be effected without too much disturbance of the clothes or of the subject's modesty, if she or he is properly garbed. To concentrate on one's task is most important. I believe that the mind's intention makes itself known to other minds in ways that are mysterious, but which I believe are conducted through the magnetic field that unites the spheres with all living things. Thus, in treating Marie Thérèse, I often closed my eyes to sense these matters more intensely and felt deeply connected to her in that double darkness—hers and mine—which we shared at such moments, a darkness which enabled me to see not only my own treatment, but the two of us from a remote distance as tiny exemplars of the forces which I was bringing to bear on her disturbance.

Her eyes were now clear, their restlessness and twitches diminished. They seemed to grow larger as the orbital muscles relaxed, allowing them to take their natural place among her other features. At times they were steady and level in their gaze, though that gaze itself harvested nothing. It was somewhat unsettling to have those eyes alight upon me, regard me steadily, at times unblinkingly, while all they saw, as it were, was the sound of my voice. At such times it was easy to convince myself that the eyes were doing their work but that the mind behind them had cut off their evidence before it could pass through her internal darkness. How disconcerting that gaze was! As I became used to it, I discovered that its strangeness arose from two matters. First, the eyes did not focus exactly at the proper distance, but seemed to look beyond me; and secondly, they were always a trifle off the mark, left or right, up or down. It is the instinct of all animals, including ourselves, that we find and lock into each other's gaze. I am always amazed at the way our two dogs unerringly meet my eyes to read my intentions. Children

do this too, and we constantly look and un-
look at each other as we talk, making or break-
ing the connection between us as our gazes
slip and meet in accompaniment to our verbal
transactions. In the extensive territory between glimpse and stare, how much is com-
municated! How much is added to our words
by the emphasis and expression of the eyes
and how they instruct our silences as we observe each other. No wonder the instinct to
observe the other's sight is so deep, thus dou-
bling our sense of ourselves, and thus of them.
I think of the four partners at the Emperor's
tennis courts, the ball as sight itself, traveling
back and forth between the doubled partners.
So it seems to me when two people meet and
immediately begin that game of tennis with
their eyes as glances travel slowly, or brutally
fast, for the impact of a stare is almost like a
slap. And how difficult it is to catch the eyes
of some! The female sex, of course, make a
game of this, as their aim seems to be to look
but not to be caught looking, leading to that
game of glances which is one of the court's
main amusements. How much the ladies seem
to gather from the briefest glimpse, those
quick darts that escape our detection. We feel
them alight upon us, but when we quickly try

to confirm them we meet only a diverted gaze. From all of this, the stare of authority to the lowered eyes of submission, Marie Thérèse was excluded. My disquiet under her apparent regard was partly due to the complete absence of expression in her eyes.

It was those very eyes, however, that gave me my next direction. For after some weeks of treatment, during which she progressively became calmer, more confident, and less disturbed by her parents' visits (which I now allowed only to reassure the parents), the eyes began to screw themselves into wrinkled pits. For a day or two I thought this was a relapse. But when she began to cover her eyes with the heels of her hands and avert her face, I realized that the treatment had made a huge advance. The fluids had begun to flow into a preliminary harmony, and I thanked my stars that their influence was so manifest. The light was hurting her eyes.

I immediately removed both of us to the large inner room with the mirrors and heavy draperies and continued the treatments in twilight, contriving to have the music played not in the same room but two rooms away, so that its sound came gently to the ear, coaxing it into attention. In that twilight, I had my great triumph.

The pain of the light was itself a kind of blindness, albeit a new blindness. The first indication of any return of her sight was Marie Thérèse's ability to discern movement when I passed an object before her eyes, which left her without any notion of the object itself. This frightened her. Indeed it would frighten anyone. To perceive a twilight full of unknown shapes and masses at different rates of movement would cause me anxiety. Sometimes those figures of motion were her own self reflected in the mirrors on each wall, particularly in the largest, over the mantel from which the ormolu clock spoke its quarters, with the tangle of cherubs climbing up its sides to the garlanded urn at its pinnacle. I had the room cleared of occasional tables and furniture, leaving only a few guiding pieces to facilitate her learning of this new space. My servant Hans, usually so reliable, moved one of the pieces to what he considered a more advantageous position without telling me, and after Marie Thérèse stumbled into it and fell, she began weeping and beating her eyes with the thumb and forefinger side of her fists. I rebuked him excessively, which he received with a dignity that made me ashamed. I then realized the extent of my nervousness with respect to this cure. And pursuing that further, I found myself further ashamed. For it was not only Marie Thérèse's welfare that concerned me, but my own. A famous patient—I think one could call her that—under the protection of the Empress, who had awarded her father a pension to nourish and protect her talents, whose malady had baffled the leading specialists of our day, one of whom was my former professor. When I shared these thoughts with my wife, she neither confirmed nor denied them but, as is her habit, said nothing while wearing her neutral smile, which I often find helpful but on this occasion did not.

Even with the few pieces of furniture in the twilit room, Marie Thérèse began to fall more frequently, though she had fully learned their position. She had always surprised me with her facility of movement after a brief learning period. But now she seemed to have unlearned the room. Her mental state, which had slowly developed into a delightful calm, began to be ruffled. I watched these changes with concern but with some understanding. I had developed a habit of talking to her from my red high-backed chair with the wings. My voice alone, I discovered, could induce that calm and confidence which made her body more receptive to the movement of the magnetic fluid. Molding and shaping the fluid with my hands was now a device which I kept in reserve. When her condition became acute, I would point my finger at the spot between her eyes, and her shivering and twitches would immediately cease despite the fact that she could not see my finger. I noticed that when I used my wand—which served as a magnetized extension of my body, arm, and finger—she occasionally followed its movements with her eyes, not directly, but *in the mirror*. But such moments were brief since, though the room was darkened, the dim light began to cause her pain. It was now difficult to examine her eyes in the light. I thus covered her eyes with a triple bandage, which I unwound to the point where she could bear the light, or what there was of it.

Often finding myself in a darkness which remained even when my eyes had become accustomed to it, I was astonished that she would find the light too harsh, even with two turns of the bandage. I took this as evidence that not only the light in the room but her own inner light was reaching her eyes, and that the fluids were flowing in accordance with the harmonies that would balance her disturbance. Yet the pain of the light frequently caused her to retreat to her own darkness. Nothing more clearly shows the delicacy of the balance of the fluids, of the necessity for the fluids to be in perfect harmony in each body, so that its health can manifest itself. How fragile and tentative is all life until it is brought into the grand harmony that joins its individual existence to the ebb and flow of the great forces that move the stars and planets.

So as Marie Thérèse and I made that darkened room a center on which the celestial rays converged invisibly, I felt acutely those powers which can be called upon by anyone whose magnetic gifts (and they vary with each person as any faculty or endowment does) are developed. I had no doubt now that we would succeed, and I say *we* advisedly, since I believe that the magnetic doctor is only the agent of forces which the patient mobilizes within, thereby being put in a position to cure himself. After the first dawn of light in Marie Thérèse, events surpassed each other in astonishment. I saw nothing less than the birth of sight itself. And while witnessing that miracle, which I witnessed before in the case of Franzl, much remains mysterious to me about the nature of sight.

I began to show Marie Thérèse various objects in the low light. My aim was not that she name them, for how could she name what she had never seen? But rather that she make a distinction between them, that she recognize that one was not the other. Simple though this may sound, she frequently mistook a snuffbox for a watch, a pipe for a Meissen figure. Language indeed became clumsy in our pursuits, for having no names to attach to the objects, she would say—it's like the last one, or it's like the one you showed me yesterday, or the day before, I don't remember. A little family of objects grew on the table, which became to her a forest of confusion. I was somewhat confused myself. I did not press upon her the names of each. To do so, I felt, would be to overtax her memory, since each object is surrounded by a hundred names in different languages, to each of which the object itself is indifferent, the object and its name being two different orders of existence, connected only by common agreement and memory. My concern was that she learn differences in shape and outline as do children when they grasp and clutch. Indeed, like a child, Marie Thérèse sometimes applied the object to her mouth, as if her lips were more informative than her eyes. I presented her with two objects at the same time, asking her to describe the differences between them. The difficulties she experienced in this simple task amazed me. Frequently Marie Thérèse would close her eyes and rotate the objects in her hands before responding coherently. When I insisted that she keep her eyes open, her hesitation, indeed confusion, became notable. The hesitation between her vision and her language became more pronounced. She did not have a convenient language for shape, though smooth and rough were no difficulty. Knowing the cunning and sensitivity of her fingers as lacemaker and pianist, I was confounded by the way the eyes lessened the information from the fingers, instead of augmenting it, as I had expected. Since we were making slow progress with shape, I assembled some patches of color and presented them to her.

The difficulties persisted. She had no names for red or blue or yellow or green. Red seemed to cause her pain, and as for the blue, she tried to put her finger not on but through it, as if I were holding a piece of sky in my hand. She made no distinction between green and yellow, and when she did perceive a difference, had no words to express it. At such moments she lost her maidenly grace and, childlike, made simple noises and gestures. Indeed, where her vision was concerned, she was a child, and I was overwhelmed with the difficulties of bringing that child to maturity in a few weeks or months. It became clear to me that curing the blindness, restoring her sight, was a most complex matter, involving a relearning of language, the world, and of space, the new medium in which she now moved in the darkened room so unsurely. I was also made aware of the detrimental effect her rudimentary sight was having on her other senses. Her touch became confused, her hearing became paradoxical, responding now to the slightest noise, now ignoring what to me seemed unusually loud. Her mouth became an elusive zone. Frequently, when feeding, she would attempt to pass the food through her cheek or chin, much to her frustration. Again and again, when in such difficulty, she would close her eyes, returning to that secure darkness in which she had negotiated fifteen years of her life so successfully.

This extreme sensitivity of her eyes did not

make our task any easier. For instance, when showing her an object or a color, she frequently identified the *succeeding* object as the one previous to it. This happened so persistently that it dawned on me that the image of an object so burned itself into her retina that she still saw it a quota of time after its withdrawal. It took a long minute for the object—feather, ring, box—to fade from her sight; if I showed her another in less than that interval, she could not see it. Indeed as the previous image faded and the other I held before her emerged, she must have been even more confused as one object was born out of another. She now closed her eyes between objects, watching, against her closed lids, the afterimage fade into darkness. While she learned to distinguish objects and colors to some extent, the room itself, bare though it was of furniture (to facilitate her movement), remained strange to her. Its walls seemed to her an immense distance away—as far as the planets—and the piano, which stood before the curtained window, she did not recognize beyond a negative pool of darkness.

On February 9th, I removed the bandages and presented myself to her imperfect sight—the first being she had seen (if seeing it was) since the onset of her malady at the age of three. What memories she had of sight or light I could never elicit. Any attempt to recover that lost paradise only added to her confusion, certain though I was that such memories would assist her now. Standing before her, no more than a meter away, I slowly moved my hands and arms, and fixed on my face a reassuring smile. We both stood, face to face, in the twilight. Her response was to cover her face and shrink from me as if she had seen something that aroused her disgust. Only when I spoke to her was she reassured, though it was a shock to her that my voice issued from the apparition which she now studied from between her fingers, covering and uncovering her eyes. In my concern, I moved closer to her and gazed solicitously into her eyes—so innocent of the world—speaking reassuringly all the while. To my surprise, she burst into laughter. Not knowing the source of another's laughter is, of all things, most irritating.

I joined in the laughter, witlessly. Marie Thérèse pointed at me, and since the distance between us was so small, and her estimate of distance so insecure, she poked her finger into my face. When I opened my eyes, she had fixed on my nose. Having located this feature, she redoubled her laughter, which in a lady of breeding (which she was) with no impairment of vision would be more than rude. Not only did she lay her finger on my nose, but she pushed it from side to side, to her further merriment, if not to mine. For, giving thought to my nose, a feature we carry without much thought about its nature, I did not find it unusual or an object worthy of mirth. It may not be sufficiently Grecian for poor Winckelmann to admire, but it has served me well these forty years and more, and sufficed to divide my eyes from each other and from my mouth in unexceptional fashion. With both her hands, she urged me to move my head from side to side, while her eyes imperfectly focused on my nose, the movement of which caused her further amusement.

Relieved as I was to hear her laugh, and pleased as I was to be the source of such a new emotion, I was greatly puzzled. When I removed the bandages the following day, the same scene was repeated, and the following day, until my nose provoked only a mild amusement. The answer was borne home to me only after the deepest reflection. Marie Thérèse had no idea of a face. Instead she saw its most prominent feature, complete in itself and unrelated to those around it. The environs of the nose, its setting, were not part of her awareness. Thus isolated, noses can indeed be comical, as I found when I tested the idea at several subsequent gatherings. This way of seeing, infantile as it must be, was Marie Thérèse's first introduction to the visible world, which causes us few surprises but which to her was full of frights and amusements unknown to the rest of us. She saw another world from mine (ours), and I puzzled as to how I might best assist her to see several separate things as they contributed to a familiar configuration rather than seeing one detail and then another and another. Thus decomposed, the objects of her sight jostled each other as unfamiliar fragments thrown up in a chaotic sea, in which near and far reversed themselves from glance to glance. This, it seemed to me as she wandered precariously around the darkened room, her eyes unbandaged, was a dangerous affliction, and I did not wonder that her new-born sight was for her more a terror than a blessing.

Patience is a primary virtue in treating those we wish to succor. Improvements can be so minute, and periods of no apparent improvement stretch without an encouraging sign, that we must believe deeply in our end and in our method. Given the improvements so obvious even to the most prejudiced observer, I had full confidence in my method. The case of Franzl and my tour of Germany had indeed confirmed both for myself and others the validity of my ideas and my application of them to individual cases. But this did not prevent me despairing at such sights as Marie Thérèse swooning at the sight of her dearest woman friend (indeed she did not believe it really was her friend), or her extreme shyness at meeting—or rather seeing—visitors whom in her darkened state she would have met with equanimity. She found humankind oddly shaped and without attraction. What grotesques she must have thought us, composed of strange details she saw with great clarity, confused by edges and borders constantly altered by the fashions of those who visited her. She found the trains of the ladies who visited her absurd, and though she knew in her mind that clothes were fitted and draped on the figure, her eyes led her to believe that the train was part of their persons, and a sliding and unpleasant part to boot. The tall headgear of the ladies, shaped like beehives and draped with veils, she rejected since they diminished the head, which she now recognized as a feature common to all, a small pedestal bearing a disproportionate load, although proportions may not accurately represent her perception, since it implies a comparative standard I was convinced she did not yet possess. However she came to the conclusion, I thought she showed good sense and I took her comment about the relation of the two—headdress and head—as a promising sign of discrimination.

People were not to her taste, but the sight of our dog, Prater (so called since he made free with so many of its trees), excited her affectionate approval. She found the dog far superior in form and grace to its owners, and later, in the park, when she saw dogs being walked, she remarked on how surely the dogs led the scarecrows behind them, under the impression that the dogs took their masters for a walk, and controlled their itinerary. Dogs indeed never failed to excite her affection and she took to hugging and kissing those that visited us in the company of their owners, often finding the owner so lacking in beauty as to be repulsive to her. This I felt to be a passing eccentricity, for I could not entertain the idea of its persistence. Being ambitious for my patient, I naturally anticipated that the full relief

of her disabilities would lead to a happy marriage, if, as the cynics doubt, such there be,
though I have seen some. Her passion for dogs
seemed a displacement of natural feelings for
the opposite sex, an opinion not discouraged
by her preference for male over female dogs.
At times this caused embarrassment for my
wife and myself when some dog, finding his
advances reciprocated, mistook her in turn for
a member of his own species, and, mounting
her extended foot or limb, proceeded to pump
on it with happy vigor, smiling, panting, and
looking around for approval all the while. The
poor girl, witless as to the dog's aim and mis-
taking his enthusiasm, would encourage him
with little cries, meanwhile calling on others
to witness this display of affection. The dog's
owner would be confused between ignoring
the scene and offering stern remonstrances to
the dog, which the girl protested prettily. Her
sight was still far from clear; at her moments
of greatest enjoyment, her pupils would roll
up, leaving only the whites, and the scene was
odd enough to press itself on the attention of
visitors who were trying to ignore both this
phenomenon and the misbehavior of their
dogs. Her affection for these animals was constantly on display. When we took our walks

outside, they seemed to know that here was someone vulnerable to their advances, for we often gathered a motley train of dogs, large and small, some trailing leashes.

But more astonishing to me were her meetings with herself in the mirrors of our darkened room. How many times did I watch her silently, seating myself in the darker shadows of that room. When I would remove the bandage from her eyes, she would flinch, then gradually accustom herself to the crepuscular twilight. If you have ever watched a swimmer dawdle under water, or a newborn foal attempting to stand—or some such beginning—you will have an idea of the quality of her motion, which combined something from each of these models. She often looked at herself piece by piece, particularly her hands, which she held very close to her eyes, no more than ten centimeters, a distance that would blind you or me. After studying them closely back and front she would pass them down the front of her dress, over her bosom and sometimes down to her thighs, bending over to stroke them, or rather the fabric covering them. She would also disengage a few strands of her hair and pull them forward to study in the same near way. She would then pick up, after a few passes at the object, a snuffbox or a Meissen figurine (which I valued, but let her have), and bring it to her face in that close scrutiny. On a whim, I placed some miniatures on the table beside her and she studied their tiny details with that intense near gaze, then reported back on every detail, not by name but by description as her language attempted to isolate its object. The hair was, in her recently acquired geography, "on top of," but she could not find the word for "head," so she touched her own hair and then pointed to the painting, which I withdrew rapidly since she was about to poke it rather than stop short. She had a similar difficulty in finding words to go with the other components of the face, whether neck or ear or lip—which for the rest of us would be a common name. What the word "face" covered for the rest of us, lapsed, in Marie Thérèse's gaze, into a concatenation of separate details.

As she rose from the chair and unsteadily found her way in the dim light, I was astonished at what the rest of us take for granted but which for Marie Thérèse was completely foreign, a matter of the most tentative learning. What she was learning, in her passage through the room, reflected in the mirrors, were two matters: her own body and the space it described in her testing and searching. She would come close to the mirror, study her face in detail, attempt to put her finger on the face in the mirror; she would carefully and insecurely back up, then come forward again, watching herself increase and diminish. It occurred to me that she had no idea of her size and must have had the uncomfortable, indeed terrifying, feeling that her size was subject to enlargement and shrinkage. Her reflections, as I have said, fascinated her. She gradually learned to identify herself in opposing mirrors as a corridor of persons, diminishing into infinity—but far from frightening her, this phantom train engaged her pleasant curiosity as she made it sway and bow to her fancy. Sometimes she played with her partner in the mirror, lifting an arm, elbow first, in slow motion, and studying her partner's response with interest. She raised both arms far above her head, stretched them to their limits on either side, and then brought them forward as if to embrace herself. Then she would approach the mirror to study her own face with such intensity that even I could be excused for confusing her image with herself as she and herself steadfastly fixed their eyes on each other, eyes which I now noticed were of a hazel color, with fine, new-grown lashes and elegant, somewhat heavy lids that had survived the insults offered them by my predecessors.

I increased the light each morning by drawing the curtains back a little more. Her eyes were now covered with only one turn of the bandage. I introduced a few more objects into the room to encourage her navigation of the ocean of space into which sight had delivered her. Gradually I stretched the time when she practiced into late afternoon and early evening. She took to sitting by the window on the second floor and looking out over the street. She did not remark on the carriages, cries, and bustle but on the song of the birds, the swallows, finches, and inevitable profusion of pigeons that populated the trees outside the window. Sometimes a swift would streak past the window, and she would flinch as if it had drawn a line across her eyeball.

All the while, I continued my treatment, passing my hands, from behind, across her brow and temples, massaging outward from the outer corner of her eyes which produced in her a kind of nodding as the fluids of the eye came into harmony with those of her body, and those of her body with the tides of magnetic force which guide the poles of our

persons into sympathy with the great con-
cordances that govern the planets. All in all,
I was most encouraged.

I now decided to dispense with the bandage
altogether, leaving her eyes open to the night,
to court sleep of their own free will. This led
to a profound shock, and then to one of my
greatest satisfactions. It was an early spring day
when the air was as clear as a lens. I had left
Marie Thérèse sitting by the window, rocking
gently forward and back as was her habit, with
a slight smile that made its appearance whenever she sat by the window. A few hours
passed before my servant Hans came running
into my room, shouting, as much as his good
manners would allow him: "Mademoiselle P.!
Mademoiselle P.!" I rushed to the room,
where my wife had preceded me. I quickly
displaced her to discover that Marie Thérèse
was gazing at the darkening sky, rocking back
and forth with great agitation, uttering groans
more animal than human, very tragic in their
tone.

It was that time of day when the light, having decided to fade, does so very quickly.
Marie Thérèse gazed at the sky with eyes so
open that I could see white above and below
her pupils. She remained insensible to me and

continued her lament. Confused and puzzled as to what accident had caused this relapse, I quickly stroked her temples and forehead, closed her eyes (which led to further wailing), then gently opened them while I attempted to balance the fluids to relieve her distress and make her sensible to my voice. Her first words were "Blind! Blind! Blind!"

This so startled me that I was sure some calamity had deprived her of her sight at its moment of rebirth. I saw in one swift prospect her darkened future, her angry parents, a displeased Empress, and the satisfaction of my colleagues. The girl was to be shown to the Empress the following week, displaying to the court my miracle. I had a precious and much-loved object in my care, a girl whose depth of character and sweetness had aroused in me a deep paternal affection. "The light! The light!" she screamed, giving me a momentary sense that all was well. "The light has gone from my eyes!" Nothing showed in her eyes; they were as translucent and clear as an angel's as far as I could see them in that darkness. And in that darkness a light burst upon me. She had never seen the night.

How simple this answer was once you knew it! With her eyes unbandaged for the first time,

Marie Thérèse had seen the night fall, and in her innocence thought that the light was fading not from the world but from her own eyes. How careless of me not to have anticipated this! I called for lights. She wept as the lamps restored her sight, and I explained that for all the world, darkness follows light and the light the darkness in that harmony of the spheres of which her own sleep was but a reflection. "Even a blink," I told her, "even that involuntary shudder of the lids, is a darkness which freshens and gilds the sight. In the brightest light we have these split seconds of darkness which, like the half-notes on the piano, have their own rhythm and quavers." This brought a smile, or the beginnings of one. I sent my wife and the servants to bed, and we remained up while I explained the night. Eventually I led her back to her seat at the window, and fixed her attention on the night sky. It was a clear night. The sounds of the city were stilled, except for the distant rumble of a coach and the occasional bark of a watchdog. I extinguished all the lights in the room behind us. I began to speak of the harmonies, the subtle movements of the fluids, how their attractions and repulsions are replicated in the harmonies of our inner organs—heart and lungs, liver and

stomach, bile and kidneys, brain and genera-
tive bodies; how all our five senses partake of
this balance, as the blood courses through our
veins, stealing to its quiet appointments in our
interior darkness, where our mind's eye can
follow.

I don't know how much she heard of this.
When she spoke I was quite startled. Her face
was turned towards the sky, a dim radiance
illuminated it. I could not see her features.
But her voice was of one seeing a vision, and
indeed she was. "The stars!" she said, "the
stars!" Above us, over the darkened house opposite, the stars seemed very close. I identified
the Great Bear, and Orion's belt and the
Pleiades. None of this she heard. "The stars
. . . the stars . . . the stars," she repeated in
wonder and delight. Nothing she had seen
since her darkness lifted had so enthralled her.
Her face in starlight glimmered like that of a
ghost without features, so that I, who do not
imagine things, felt a shiver. Several thoughts
came to me. To her imperfect vision, the stars
may have seemed close enough to reach out
her hand and touch them. Or they could be,
to my fancy, *inside* her eyes. As I looked up
with her, and through her eyes, I had another
fancy—that the stars were pinholes in a great

dark sheath, behind which was a blaze of eternal light.

Turning back to watch her, I requested her not to be disturbed by my close scrutiny. Her pupils were not fixed or still, but moved across the firmament as if these spheres were a harmony to which her whole being responded. In my imagination, I could see in the globes of her eyes the tiny reflections of the constellations. It was a moment that led to such fancies and a moment to be remembered all my life. My reverie was interrupted by her voice, gentle and girlish again: "The stars are the most beautiful sight that I have seen since I could see."

Eventually I persuaded her that she must sleep, and not wishing to disturb the servants, disturbed my wife, not to her immediate pleasure, to see Marie Thérèse to bed. Each night she now returned to the window and the night sky, and it was often difficult to persuade her to her bed. How short-lived such pure and exalted joy would be!

———— ·*3*· ————

ou must write exactly as I tell you, for I have no way of seeing what I write, and when you read it back to me it seems, by your emphasis, different from my intention. You have always been patient and tried to repair such matters to bring them closer to my intention. But in this double dark- ness that I have suffered—which is not alto-

gether unpleasant—I can tell much by the way
a person speaks, what little meanings build
upon their words over and above the words
themselves. So I wish my own voice to be as
accurate to the facts as I can manage. And in
this, as in so much else, I need your gracious
help.

Versions of my story fly around Europe like
courtiers eager to please King Curiosity. The
infirmities of my flesh, fainting fits and such,
are always welcome news to those who wish
to diminish my name or see me as a kind of
performing dog, remarkable because I can do
what one in my state should not be able to do.
Add to this that I am a woman, and therefore
not serious by most men's definition, and you
will see how eager I am to clarify those events
which have given rise to so much gossip. Who
knows these events better than I, who is the
darkness at their center? And who can better
tell truth from falsehood than I, who have
heard the conflicting voices argue my fate and
future, even as they betray their thoughts by
the way their words are spoken?

When Dr. Barth came to visit, to test my
new-found sight, it was in that large mirrored
room, the shape and dimensions of which I
will always remember with the deepest plea-

sure. In that room, adjacent to the small bed-
room on the second floor, I met the light.
Unlike the previous visit of my old doctor,
Dr. Stoerk, and his colleagues, Dr. Barth's
visit was not benign. Dr. Barth, I am told,
specialized in treating cataract, and he examined my eyes extremely closely, with the intention, it seemed to me, of finding his
speciality in them. I am often asked what I can
tell from voices, since my judgment of their
owners has been proved correct more often
than not. In Dr. Barth's voice, and later in that
of his friend Dr. Ingenhousz, I heard a contradiction, a wish to please, then to hurt my
beloved Dr. Franz. He was present, of course,
and their voices, when they addressed me and
then him, varied in a manner that made me
uneasy, not for myself but for my dear doctor.

I have always been one who, to my cost,
picks up the nervousness of others, much as
some people will catch a cold from another a
street away. Their nervousness seems to express itself in my person, and though I have
been aware of this since I became a woman,
it does not help me withstand this infection of
my emotions. Thus I have gathered, unfairly
in my opinion, a reputation for temperament
which, while useful to a degree, leads some to

believe me incapable of handling my affairs.
You who have been my friend and amanuensis,
indeed my eyes, know how false this is. But
it is the habit of the world to fit the truth to
its own idea of it, whatever distortions may
result. I do not deny my infirmity, which I
never think of as my dead eyes but as that
infection of the emotions I catch from others,
especially those near to me, as my parents will
testify. I learned, as a young girl, to have patience with the procession of people who came
to prod my eyes, purge and bleed me, shock
my eyeballs with the new electricity and generally torment me in ways which, if not sanc-
tioned by the medical profession, would make
its members liable to prosecution. The good
doctors produced in me more sickness, pain,
and disease than my poor body was ever guilty
of before their ministrations. Indeed it is a joke
among the courtiers that to be a king on his
deathbed is to invite the most exquisite tortures, which, the wits say, reconciles their majesties to leaving the world as nothing else
could.

How different is the good doctor Franz!
How elevated and noble are his harmonies, all
the more so to me, whose life has been to
transfer to others, in my way, the harmonies

of those composers I so deeply admire, and most of all the works of my dear Wolfgang, who is scarcely more than a few years older than myself. Besides such elevated things, Dr. Barth's questions seem to issue from a small room with small windows.

It had been the practice of my beloved Dr. Franz to make a little gathering of objects on the occasional table beside my chair. He started with one or two—a miniature, a Meissen figurine, and once, as a kind of joke, a pipe, which was a great mystery to me until I smelled it. Over the months, the table supported a puzzlement of objects, some of which he changed each day to surprise me. Though I could see the objects in a general way, I found it difficult to separate their shapes, different though these objects were. The good doctor insisted that I keep my eyes open when I held them, because my habit was to close my eyes, at which time the objects would become familiar, no longer an enigma but a glass cube, a snuffbox, a tiny animal in bronze. Yet when I opened my eyes, the meaning or sense of the object often fled, leaving me with a strange object in my hand. My confusion is hard to imagine for those whose eyes confirm their other senses by habit. I must have tried the

patience of the good doctor sorely, particularly
on one occasion when he allowed my mother,
at her request, to stay. Her annoyance at what
she thought my stupidity confused me further,
so that I began to shake, and the doctor's kind
wife was called in to divert my mother and
lead her away. But all this was nothing to the
ways of Dr. Barth.

He picked up an object from the side table
and asked me to name it without asking, as
Dr. Franz would have, if I saw it first. I
reached for the object—I still do not know
what it was to this day—but he would not let
me touch it. The shape of things was the most
difficult for me, and it was with the assistance
of touch that I learned to place a name on what
presented itself, however imperfectly, to my
sight. But Dr. Barth would have none of it. If
I did not know the name, how could I say I
knew the object?

The name to me was not the object, and had
as little relation to it as the name of the next
object. Objects do not smell of their names as
do flowers of their perfumes. Having thus be-
wildered me, I misnamed several objects, Dr.
Franz told me later. I called a small china dish
a pipe, a figurine I mistook for a snuffbox, and
a heavy ring that Dr. Barth had taken from his

finger and offered me became, in my confusion, a pair of spectacles. At times, Dr. Barth
persisted in holding my attention to the same
object, and after my failure to name it, proceeded to ask me what it was like, provoking
me to engage in wilder guesses. He then reversed himself, asking me to name what it was
not, prompting a set of answers which were
simply names to me—button, earring, toy
mouse—in the hope that one would fit. He did
not hold the object still but tilted it in such
ways that it became several objects, as if he
held a magic set of transformations in his hand
like a conjurer. He nodded wisely all the time,
as if my answers confirmed his predisposition.
To my distress was added the feeling that I
had disappointed Dr. Franz, though in truth
he never gave me any indication of this, then
or after. As I listened to the polite argument
that followed, over by the high window, between Dr. Franz and his visitor, I was struck
by how firm and reasonable Dr. Franz remained as Dr. Barth declared me blind because I could not name the simplest things.
Dr. Franz responded that as one who had
never seen them before, how could I name
them? In addition he lectured Dr. Barth on
the difficulties of finding my way about with

what he called "a stranger's body in a foreign place," by which he meant, I suppose, this room in which I had recovered my sight. Dr. Barth distressed and confused me to such an extent that he drew a quiet word of caution from Dr. Franz, which provoked Dr. Barth to say that he did not need lessons in how to approach patients. They fell to arguing and I to shaking, much as I would have liked not to admit to Dr. Barth his effect upon me.

Up to this time my life with Dr. Franz had been full of light and wonders, the terrors of which he had patiently led me through. For those months, I lived in two worlds, one of comfortable darkness, the other of exhilaration and confusion. My parents' visits, which were few, did not disturb me. I took a great liking to Dr. Franz's wife and she, I think, to me. Her aspect was at all times calm and pleasant, very different from my own mother, who enlarged every trifle to a magnitude beyond her capacity to cope with it. I was also relieved that my father, whom I loved dearly, kept at a distance; from my earliest years he had sternly urged me to the harpsichord, demanding long hours of practice, which, with time, I came to enjoy. When he did visit, he insisted that I play for him.

Dr. Franz's house was, above all, calm. Rarely did I meet or hear of other patients. Three or four times I heard distant screams, but they were cut off abruptly, as if a heavy door had closed upon them. My imagination made much of this until Frau M. explained that I had overheard a crisis, when the fluids rushed through the body in a tumult before settling down in harmony with the spheres. When I heard such cries thereafter, animal and desperate though they seemed, I was much consoled, hearing them now not as extreme distress but as the stormy doorway through which the sick passed into health. I understood a little of this, since when my distress at the light and its confusions caused me to shake and sob, my despair would be succeeded by a satisfactory calm, which returned more quickly when I closed my eyes. Indeed darkness and light drew me towards them in different ways. Suspended between both, I sought a satisfactory twilight where the lessons of darkness would sustain me as I coped with the terrors of light.

Before Dr. Barth's visit, Dr. Franz had taken me out of the house to the garden and shown me further marvels. As we strolled down the garden path, I noticed that the sides

of the path, or rather the trellis that confined
it on either side, moved with us in a way that
reminded me of the rapid tick of a French
clock, a clock which stopped when I stopped
and accompanied me when I moved again. The
motion of things always surprised me, for the
world was never still but always in motion,
whether by itself or in response to my movement. What was close moved constantly, what
was far away moved as stealthily as a mouse.
Near and far so confounded me that my idea
of them was often reversed. Thus the trees in
the Prater, on the far bank of the Danube,
seemed to me miniatures which I could grasp
in my hand, though when I reached for them
my hand loomed like that of a monster. When
I reached for what was near to me, my hand
often searched the air around it as if my hand
itself were blind. Yet I saw objects as clearly
as I heard every sound. When I held them
close to my eyes, they seemed to recede from
me and appear as they do in dreams, which I
began to have increasingly as Dr. Franz
treated me. In these dreams I saw myself
stumbling in terror over unseen objects, holding small things which turned into large, unable to recognize what I saw, and from these
dreams I would wake up in great fear. But in

my dreams the figure of Dr. Franz began to appear, standing in the distance at the mouth of a cave, beckoning me to come out of the darkness, so that even as my body suffered and stumbled, my mind went towards him and I forced my eyes to remain open.

To my distress, the confusions that Dr. Barth had aroused did not settle. Before his visit, Dr. Franz had talked of how I would demonstrate at court the progress I had made, playing for the Empress. I would walk unaided to the harpsichord, and when I reached it, would slowly turn and return the audience's stare, my eyes dancing from one member to another like a butterfly (as Dr. Franz put it). Soon after Dr. Barth's visit, I heard no more of this, and began to wonder if Dr. Franz himself had begun to lose confidence in me. He gave no evidence of this, continuing our walks in the garden, instructing me in the difference between near and far. To me the Danube looked like a white ribbon that I could reach out and pick up. It had no character of water that I could see.

There were times when I felt my learning was advancing steadily. I had a good notion of colors, and began to place their names more accurately on the colored patches Dr. Franz held up to me. Objects remained mysterious. While I had no difficulty whatever in seeing something as it moved towards me, it was only after I touched it—to give an example—that I recognized the house cat. Yet this knowledge did not convey itself from hands to eyes, for I made the same mistake a few days later. I was like a person with two languages (I have French in addition to my native German), one which put the world into reasonable order, the other which bore no relation to the world at all.

What I saw and what I heard were thus distracted, and the glory of the light, which I had welcomed with awe and gratitude, began to seem a doubtful blessing, one which I could, of course, eclipse by closing my eyes. At times, when I walked out with Dr. Franz, the movements and colors, and my own movements within those movements, became so bewildering that although I forced myself to keep my eyes open, I saw nothing but a confused madness that made me tremble. Of my two forms of blindness, you can imagine which I suffered more gladly.

My father now visited more often, and his joy in my cure seemed diminished. When my parents fell into a mood, I always presumed

that I was the cause, and so had a habit of
feeling guilty. I always felt my dead eyes were
a burden to them. Indeed anyone in my condition would probably share my feeling. The
possessors of full sight can never understand.
No matter how tender, they often seem obtuse
and never more so than when they ask me their
most common question: "What can you not
see?" The answer being, of course, that if I
could see, I could tell them. What they cannot
know is my sightlessness. Their world is different from mine, as is that of my beloved
parents, whose joy at my cure was at first so
unbounded. The recent months have, I'm
sure, been difficult for them. They have had
to become accustomed to another daughter,
whose new sight so altered her at times that
they must have felt me replaced by another
person, as indeed I often felt myself to be.

Like all my own species, my parents were
curious to my sight, discernible as father and
mother only when they spoke, or when their
step approached. I continued to have great
difficulty in distinguishing one person from another. My parents now made their visits together, and while they spoke to me kindly, if
somewhat artificially, they would then fall to
whispering in an agitated way, withdrawn to

where I could not distinguish their words, though I was certain that I was their subject. Dr. Franz always bid them to remove themselves to another room when he came upon them at such times, which they did, until on one occasion my father refused to do so, saying he had every right to stay with his daughter as long as he wished. When Dr. Franz left, he returned to his whispered discussion with my mother, but such was their degree of disagreement that he began to shout at her, as she continued to whisper loudly to him to lower his voice or I would overhear him. At this point there was no difficulty in hearing either, and the subject of their disagreement was no secret.

My father's tones did not diminish, but drew my mother's whispers to almost the same volume—if you can imagine a whispered shout—which seemed to increase my father's distemper. The sounds of their voices confused me. When I closed my eyes, their voices issued from the corner of the room where their persons were located. But when I opened my eyes, they seemed to issue every which way, first from one place and then another, so that it seemed to me a company of mothers and fathers were arguing like furies. Though I was the subject of their disagreement, my cries and sobs were ignored. A servant sent for Dr. Franz, who quickly arrived, consoled me in his arms, and ordered my mother and father to cease their disagreement or leave at once.

My father, who makes such a marvellous habit of politeness that he can return to it almost instantly, addressed Dr. Franz in a cold voice, saying that while he appreciated his ministrations to me, he now desired to end them, since I had entered Dr. Franz's care as a mature young woman of high skills and accomplishments and was now so unsure and uncertain of myself that I was no more than a baby, and that what I needed were the familiarities of my own home. With this I did not agree, no more than did my mother, who set up a great wailing, in which I joined. My father then left abruptly, with angry footsteps, and my mother and I clung to each other in mutual agitation. As was often the case, I found myself comforting her to the point where she could assure herself she was comforting me. As the harmonies of my fluids were disturbed, my body began to betray me, and I fainted into the darkness.

When I awoke to Dr. Franz's gentle voice, I was on the sofa in the same room where he had first brought the light to my eyes; it was twilight outside and, apart from a few candles, almost dark within. It was several days before I wished to leave that room again. My father did not visit but my mother came every day. I refused to see her for several days since her presence increased my agitation, despite the fact that she supported my desire to remain with Dr. Franz. Once when she was with me, we heard Wolfgang's voice outside the door. My mother ran out to him and engaged him in conversation about the court, along with flattering words about his first use of Johann Stein's new piano, in which I myself was most interested for it issued a stronger sound than the clavichord while losing none of its delicacy.

Wolfgang, who was always in such a good humor that he was not aware of the lack of it in others, proceeded upon a long explanation, which I heard imperfectly through the door, and which I very much wanted to hear. I wished for my mother's departure, but it was not forthcoming. The clock accomplished what my desire could not, for on the noon hulla-balloo of the French ormolu, my mother, with pretty cries, excused herself that she was late for an appointment with the Empress's dress-maker, and, rushing in, kissed me a quick goodbye with her usual exhortations to behave myself. Wolfgang, as he often did, took time with me, and amused me at the clavichord, playing with that easy flow I have tried to imitate, the hands gentle but brisk so that the tones cluster, fall apart as if scattered, are gathered and urged forward again with the same lightness. He often plays something he is working on, sometimes saying, "This is as far as I've got." Then he embarks on an exhilarating confusion of notes, runs of perfectly balanced phrases, which explode into extremes of disorder, or collapse inward into intricacies I can follow only so far. "Or it could go this way," he says, making puns and jokes with repetitions of the melody or putting bass and treble in absurd conversation from the extremes of the keyboard. I watch his hands though their speed confuses me, and given my stage of recovery, they seem to me tentacled little beasts running wild on the steps of the keys. We usually end up laughing. He encourages me to play for him and listens with apparent pleasure.

I try to make the tone as transparent and pure as possible, without the dreadful banging and jingling I have heard from some others who are judged passable at the court. I am

always struck by how few know what one is
doing and how the audiences at court seem to
have their minds made up before the performance and suit their applause to this precon-
ception, unless the performance is obviously
deficient. Thus reputation plays the audience
as the performer plays the clavichord—on a
score already determined. I have spoken of
this to Wolfgang, as we have of many things
musical, including gossip. He dismisses most
performers with an enviable confidence,
which gives me confidence, for he always
seems so certain of himself. He encourages me
to play my own compositions and often shows
me how a phrase could be made more alert
with a slight change in the order or the tempo.
Then he plays it in a manner that transforms
it, and thus enhanced, hands it back to me. I
do not think my gifts, however, lie in composition, but in execution.

As the new piano persuades more musicians
of its virtues, Wolfgang says that composers
will write for it, citing himself and Clementi,
although he has differences with Clementi on
how the instrument should develop. What at-
tracts him to the new piano is how bass and
treble are so matched in it, and the way in

which the light hammers set the strings singing without that lingering vibration that trails one note into the other so that one is forced to play over an undercurrent of harmonious noise. Dr. Franz, who always knows what is happening in music, acquired one of the new pianos a few weeks after my arrival, and he encourages me to play it. Sometimes, when Wolfgang arrives, he sets the two of us to playing duets, often joining us on that strange glass harmonica of his.

These duets are the greatest joy to me, for Wolfgang drives the music along with such quickness and lightness that I feel I am flying with him. He plays little games between the notes, inserting a note or a half-note in between so that it tilts a passage in a new way, almost as if he were recomposing the work as we play it. Especially when I am playing treble, he exaggerates or plays against me in such a way that it makes both of us burst out laughing. He sometimes mocks other composers, but when he amuses himself with my dear Salieri, who has never been anything but kindness itself to me, I fall silent. He never does this when he plays Haydn, whom he reveres and who in turn reveres him. He puts great store by Haydn's opinion, as he should, since Haydn holds that Wolfgang is the first among composers.

Sitting side by side on the long stool, I am aware with Wolfgang of things that perhaps he is not. Sometimes, reaching over to the treble, his arm brushes against my bosom in a way that adds a note of pleasure to the notes that are flocking around us. I think of this more than I should, and must confess that at times I have not been disinclined to lean my bosom to where his arm must brush it. Sometimes he asks Dr. Franz to take the piano and dances me around the room, which gives me an excitement I have never experienced, and, as I close my eyes so that things do not whirl madly, he guides me as if he were my heart and eyes in one. He provokes a delicious vertigo, as if I were spiraling up and down the inside of a velvet tower. I want then to lose myself in some delirium, a mad darkness which frightens me so that I cry to Wolfgang, "Enough! Enough!" pretending to need a rest and panting from the exertion. At those moments I see such colors inside my eyes—dark mauves and purples (I may have their names wrong), sometimes marvellous blues—which bloom and fade, making a space richer than any I have known through the exercise of sight.

Sight has brought with it so many confusions that I feel like a child who must learn the simplest things. That is what Dr. Barth did not understand. I hardly understand it myself. I am often discouraged, and it is only Dr. Franz's patience that assists my own. But yesterday when Wolfgang and I were playing a duet, my unstable senses betrayed me, and I have not been the same since. Dr. Franz, since we both love music, had begun to teach me to read the notes on the page, but they quickly became a buzz of dots that made little sense. I understood the staff, an anchor to which I clung at the beginning of each line. I could distinguish the notes, like tiny insects, and, like insects, they tended to move, especially when I moved my eyes, and to twitch and jump as if alive. But this was not my main concern, for my memory for music is very well-formed, and I learn from the repetition of others, who play passages until I put together the whole, play it by rote, then find its meaning through playing it according to my pleasure and delight, or what my father calls "according to my nature."

On this occasion, while playing with Wolfgang, the sight of the notes, white and black

like so many sticks, caused my fingers to lose
their independence. This oversight took from
my hands their brains, for they are like little
trained animals who agree to join each other
in unison and counterpoint. Once you think of
your right and left hands as separate, as the
sight of them inclined me to, they began to
quarrel, leaving me no way to subdue their
disagreement. My hands began to resist my
orders, and opening and closing my eyes distressed them further. The sound they elicited
from the keyboard began to wander. It appeared to come from different places in the
room. I had not understood how the ears con-
spire to return the sound to the hands, keeping
them instructed. But with my eyes open, the
sound seemed to reach me from above, or from
behind, and even from under the piano, so
that my hands, on this uncertain testimony of
my ears, felt themselves unconnected to the
effects they were producing, and thus began
to sulk, becoming clumsy and foreign to me.
Out of these dilemmas issued a poor music.

When Wolfgang visited again, he witnessed
my hesitation and distress. We played, but I
broke our duet again and again. He cheerfully
went back to start us, but each time I could
not finish. At one such time, I saw what ap-

peared to be a figure at the door. I do not know how long he had been there. When I noticed him, he turned away immediately and left. I knew from his footsteps that it was my father.

The piano, my greatest joy, now became a torture for me, since I could not leave it alone. Dr. Franz reassured me that this difficulty would pass, but even when playing a simple piece, I repeatedly missed the change in key. I was only too quickly discomforted. I developed a habit of putting my face in the keyboard to distinguish the notes, and then began to find my face in my knuckles, which may have looked comical to some, for I heard Dr. Franz rebuke one of the maids for giggling. The more my difficulties presented themselves, the more I attempted to overcome them, which led to further frustration. The discords that I produced brought me to tears and I would slap one hand with the other to rebuke its loss of memory. For those of us who cannot see, the hands have their own memory of the music, of distance and spaces, so that the keys can be hit square and not in the seam between as I found myself doing with open eyes. My father now came several times to watch my ineptitude with a disapproval I could feel all too well. From my earliest childhood he had the ability to signify his disapproval with a silence that invaded my darkness like a fog. My mother now joined him frequently, and they resumed their arguments, adding to my troubles.

The nature of the argument was all too clear to me. My father wanted me home; the treatment was a failure. He observed that Dr. Barth's diagnosis countered that of Dr. Franz, of whom he now spoke disrespectfully even when he was in the room. He repeatedly addressed himself angrily to Dr. Franz: "The girl is now a shadow of herself. Look at her. She cannot play. She cannot see the simplest things. She understands nothing. She has become a child. Her skill is gone. She made a mockery of music the other day with that young genius you value so much. She needs her father, her home, her own life, not this conjurer's palace."

All this delivered bluntly and far from my father's usual graces. My mother tried to intercede but he would interrupt himself to shout her down. She came over to the piano, where I now often sat without playing, put her arms around me, and was brave enough to support my desire to stay with Dr. Franz, who for all the terrors he had introduced me to, had brought me wonders that would always be with me, like a glimpse through a window of a dark carriage when traveling by night. Dr. Franz was unsparing in his response to my father. "You, sir," he said, "who know so little but your own opinion of things, which, as is your habit, reflects that of others, have no true regard for your daughter's illness. She came to me wounded by the ministrations of others. Now the world is being born to her, and this new-born sight must be preciously guarded. Yes, she is in another infancy, the infancy of her sight, and it is for us to protect it, to guide it, to patiently support her spirit until the light shines through her eyes, her language, her body, her hands. You bully the sight out of her eyes, which shows to me no evidence of a father's love. The main impediment to her progress is your own person. I will not allow your presence here again. I will deliver your daughter to you fully cured, and playing the piano better than an angel."

With this my father turned on his heel (this I saw quite distinctly), saying, "You will hear from me." After a long silence, Dr. Franz began to speak gently to my mother. He spent many hours with me that evening at the high window, massaging my body, my temples and forehead, to settle the disturbed fluids that had caught up my eyes in their agitation.

Two days later, sometime towards the middle of May, my mother came again. She regretted my father's rudeness. But she was a different mother, who now supported my father's order to have me returned to them. She begged Dr. Franz to release me, as the whole business had multiplied her troubles and she had begun to wish it had never started. I was again at the piano, sitting silently, afraid to play. Dr. Franz said that if I returned home, they could not count on him. The prospect of a separation from my beloved doctor agitated me as I had not been for months. The nurse took hold of me as I began to weep and cry. My mother shrieked at me, as she had done many times when I was a child, rushed at me, half-embraced me, then flung me from her against the wall, which seemed to rise to strike me. I came to my senses in bedlam and total darkness. There was a struggle and shouts. I heard my father's voice raised in terrible anger. Dr. Franz and the servants exchanged urgent cries: "The sword! The sword!" I heard nothing from my mother, but, half rising, I tripped over her, lying on the floor. After that, all I heard were my father's curses on Dr. Franz and his "household of charlatans and fools," and thereafter I was in darkness again, which is my fate.

*E*very time I hear the name of that accursed man, a name I sent around the
courts of Europe, I could almost injure myself with vexation. As a result of his
fakery and nonsense, I was compromised at
court, I nearly lost the favor of Her Gracious
Majesty, and my daughter became a stranger
to me. Idle folk at court began to talk behind

my back, and those chamberlains, secretaries, assistants, and masters of ceremony who had always treated me with the respect due a secretary to their Majesties began to test my favor, sending my name around with nothing more attached to it than the notion that my status had diminished, as it does even when nothing weighs it but that it has become a subject for gossip.

All this when I had serious matters to think of, concerning both their Majesties. The Empress during this time was having one of her attacks of air hunger, gasping when she lay down and out of breath when she moved, due in part to her tendency towards stoutness. Dr. Stoerk was forever at the palace. She will not give up this idea of legislating public morals which, given the conduct of several at court, caused much laughter among those wits who call her group the "chastity commission." She was still quarreling with her son, the Emperor, over the partition of Poland, regretting that she had approved it; and she is again sending a storm of letters to that daughter of hers in Paris. Prussia is always on her mind and all the more so now that there is danger there. My domestic woes seem trivial compared to all this. But even in the midst of everything,

the Empress would turn to me and ask how
my daughter fared, and how she wished to
hear her play again soon. How was I to tell
her that the girl couldn't play a note because
of that man's meddling?

I was constantly on the go between her and
her son, the Emperor, rephrasing one of her
comments in a diplomatic way and similarly
translating his reply. Why they didn't talk to
each other directly is a mystery to me, and why
they chose me as envoy only partly pleased
me, for they used me to go around Von Kaunitz, who will never even give me a glance, so
full is he of important matters conducted over
my little head. When there is anything important it is Von Kaunitz here, Von Kaunitz there;
as for matters entrusted to me, they are usually
no more than Her Majesty's complaints about
her son's French thinking and his strange admiration for her enemy, Frederick, which
everybody knows about anyway.

So each of them asks me what the other is
thinking, particularly, of course, when they
are not speaking. Like her, Joseph wants Silesia back and is willing to go to war for it, if
she will let him. She still has enough bite to
keep him from running off in his headstrong
way. Both of them are of a single mind about

the reforms that are necessary, especially land reforms, but that frightens us all. We have hardly settled on one crisis before we are dealing with the next and hearing of a third. My friends at the palace say yes to everything and then, like men of sense, delay it as much as possible. I am at my wits' end staying in favor when everyone is at odds or making sudden alliances I am ignorant of until I blunder into them, and when my advice is asked, I give it with an eye to several different consequences, and so it is ignored. Our friends now are the French and the Russians, and the Emperor is proud to ally himself with the great Catherine in our balancing acts against the Prussians. I hear talk that she will benefit more than we, so shrewd is that lady in her bargains. With all this on my mind, and the Empress increasingly unwell and spending most of her time at Schönbrunn, you can imagine my irritation at this fool's meddling, for which I have only myself to blame. Why did I let this happen?

My wife never ceased in her protestations to have that charlatan look at our daughter, and after Stoerk and, later, de Wenzel gave up on her, we were ready to try anything. Marie Thérèse, the joy of my life, had become more like her mother under the endless treat-

ments, ready to faint at any time, weeping for
no cause but her own sense of misery, which
irritated her mother out of her wits, so that
she began to scold and beat her, which provoked me greatly. It is not true that I have
treated my wife in like fashion, as you may
have heard from those vile fellows at court,
who heard it in turn from their wives, to whom
my wife exaggerates everything. She will not
keep her own council, as I tell her to, and that
damned uncle of hers, Baron de Colnbach,
took me to task about it, since he too had heard
the rumors. She does not hesitate to remind
me how much of our fortunes are owed to the
intercessions of her uncle at court.

All this would test any man's patience, and
it would take a saint not to have accompanied
my rebukes with an odd cuff at her wig, after
which she cries to the servants, goes to her
room, and faints when they arrive. It is true
that my temper is sometimes poor, but I swear
that I spared my wife any rudeness until I saw
her attack my daughter in a way that has now
become a habit when my daughter provokes
her. She catches her in her arms and throws
her to the ground with cries of lamentation
and scolding. What has she done, she cries,
to deserve such a daughter? Well may I ask

what I have done to deserve such a wife? My wife's lack of reason at these moments is so great that only a slap suffices to return her to her senses; when she arrives at them, she screams at me and I am sorely tried to refrain from repeating the medicine.

I was so sick of this howling that I resisted all her entreaties to subject my daughter to the pernicious Dr. M. For everyone has heard of the screaming and shouting—"crises" they call them—that attend his "cures," and of screaming and shouting I have had my fill. I visited with my uncle-in-law, De Colnbach, who is M.'s supporter, on just one occasion. What with music and howls mingling in a room where ladies and gentlemen (from whom one would expect better sense) sat around a great vat of water, holding pipes or some such that issue from it, it was a torment not to laugh. When the great Dr. M. entered, some of these fools begin to moan and whimper, especially the ladies. When he passed his hands over them, they went into hysterics (which my wife manages by herself without treatment) and tall silent fellows, dressed in black, gathered them up and bore them off, I know not where, as they twitched and shook giving forth animal noises of a kind quite disgusting to hear.

Where they went, or what happened to them, is plain to any man of sense. What do you think happens when powerful young men bear off hysterical ladies into what I hear are padded rooms where their screams are abruptly silenced? And some of the fancy fellows around the tub seem eager for the same treatment.

It was only desperation itself, and my wife's nagging, supported by the Baron, that induced me to test the idea of allowing M. near my daughter, but only when I satisfied myself that my daughter would not partake of the vat in the company of others, and that she would be spared those periodic rescues by the young men in black. Dr. M. agreed to all this and assured me, as did the Baron on his honor, that he would treat my daughter himself, separately, with full attention.

In only one area did Dr. M. and I converse to our mutual satisfaction, on the subject of music. For whatever his other nonsense, he does know music, and it was this, in part, that led me to trust him with my daughter. Not that we agreed on musical matters, even though I have guided my daughter with such excellent results, as all, from the Empress down, agree. He favors Gluck's fol-de-rol. I myself am partial to *Alceste*, which shows he

can have a serious side. Gluck lives down the
street from the magic doctor. It astonishes me
how much musicians think of their Dr. M.
Even Haydn is among his admirers. Haydn is
a force now, happy in his music and unhappy
in everything else; the wits say he'd have better lost his balls and sing falsetto at St. Stephen's than be married to his witch, but then,
which of us would marry if we could step
twenty years into the future for five minutes?
But it is Mozart that the great doctor talks
about all the time; he is a close friend of the
father, who never ceases to share his worries
with everyone. As for that "miraculous boy,"
Dr. M. thinks he is the superior of everyone,
and spoke to me in that silly way of his about
the boy's music echoing the spheres, as if his
works were planetary compositions. And then,
of course, more nonsense about his precious
fluids and how good music soothes them. I've
seen fluids so settle in Mozart's listeners at
court that they close their eyes and play their
own bassoons until someone gives them an
elbow before the Empress notices.

My own feeling is that the boy is a gifted
machine, like those mechanical chess players
who ring as many changes as the court ladies
have clothes. But he hasn't an ounce more to

tell me that Haydn hasn't already told me. He is misled by new-fangled ideas and the latest thing in instruments. He is raving about the new piano, which I think a vulgar instrument, lacking the delicacy of the clavichord, which, when played by a master, sounds like the delicate tearing of exquisite silks, or at least that thought sometimes comes to mind when I listen. Mozart is for every fad, and he encourages that great musician, Dr. M., to play his absurd glass harmonica, which for Haydn was just an amusement but which Dr. M. thinks is among the first of instruments, perhaps because it is based on all those fluid levels, which I suppose he magnetizes to get better music out of it. He even bought one of those new pianos, and you can imagine my distress when I made a surprise visit and found my daughter playing on it. Dr. M., of course, gave me no satisfaction, quoting Mozart that this was the instrument of the future. My answer was, let the future take care of itself; she will play with the instrument of the present. We conducted our disagreement pleasantly enough, for this was early in his treatment.

Indeed in those early days, the benefits, I will admit, were measurable. In the light of my later distemper, I have been asked why I wrote that paean of praise to Dr. M. and his "cure." I can only say I had no idea of the disasters to come. My hopes encouraged me beyond my judgment, and such was the atmosphere of that place that you would tend to believe anything you wanted to. Add my daughter's pleasure at her own improvement, and my wife's exaggeration of everything, and you will see how joyfully we allowed ourselves to be borne forward to this desolate shore. Oddly enough, one of the things that convinced me to submit my daughter for further treatment was not the recovery of her sight, however doubtful that was, but the recovery of her ability to smell. I was there when that happened.

Marie Thérèse had had another miserable night, I was informed when I arrived. It was one of those times when she empties herself inside out from top and bottom, on which occasions my wife maintains a sleepless vigil, waking me when there is some news, and sometimes when there is none. My beloved daughter's weaknesses of the flesh have been legion. Her stomach and bowels, as old Van Swieten used to say, should be reordered from the Creator. Over these afflictions, her music soared in evidence of a spirit like an angel's.

When she was at that wretched piano in the big room at M.'s, the servant came in and put a vase of flowers on the piano as she played, rubrems and roses and a few hollyhocks (where M. can procure roses in January is another of his little mysteries). An interruption in the music caught my attention; I usually listen with my eyes closed. She was pointing her nose towards the flowers and, half standing and leaning over, produced a discord on the piano by touching it with her dress, which she disregarded as she sniffed around the flowers as if locating them. Her hand followed until she found and grasped a few buds which she crushed in her fingers, then rubbed into her face, smiling joyously and proclaiming her victory. She did not say, as I would have expected, "I can smell!" but kept repeating, "The flowers! The flowers!" each time she raised her head from her hands, bits of petals sticking to her face streaked blood-red from the rubrems, which momentarily startled me. At that moment, my good feelings betrayed me to think kindly of M.'s ministrations. Indeed at that time wherever I looked, there seemed to be progress, which, of course, I reported to the Empress when taking another letter full of admonitions for her French daughter. Her Majesty, who loves my girl, allowed as how she wished to see the results when convenient, and I was much gratified by her gracious interest.

My daughter's eyes, which had bulged like a spaniel's, had then retreated to their normal eminence; she didn't tremble and sweat as she had since she lost her sight. She now responded to the light like a child to a burn, but M., whom I still believed in then, explained that this was a preface to her recovery of sight, and that the light, which she had not seen for fifteen years, was a severe insult to those tender organs. I had another encounter with M. soon after that, for according to him both my wife and I had neglected to tell him that my daughter had had perfect sight until the age of three. I explained that each of us had thought that the other had told him. Indeed I have the distinct impression to this day that I did tell him, and that it had escaped his mind. I now remember that I did tell him. I did tell him she had not been born blind. And on repeating this to him, he responded that I had kept the circumstances of her loss from him. To which I responded that these were no secret.

She woke up on the morning of the 9th of

December 1762 with no ability to see anything. He said, "How did you know she had
lost her sight?" I responded that this was all
too obvious. She had walked into the wall of
her room when we set her on her feet and had
repeated this action several times, like a mechanical toy. She did not grasp at anything
held in front of her and could not distinguish
between her dolls. She did not blink when I
waved my hand close to her eyes and a fool
could tell that something terrible had befallen
us. He pestered me with questions, insisting
that I speculate on the cause of this misfortune.
I replied that had I an idea of that, I myself
might be able to remove it. In my view, there
was no cause. She had suffered a curse that
had deprived her, and us, of the light, for she
was and is the light of my life. The clamor my
wife set up that morning still abuses my memory. She threw herself on the girl as if to force
her to see, and when unsuccessful, flung herself headlong on the ground, moaning and
weeping and terrifying my daughter, who kept
asking what was the matter with her mother.
The child herself did not seem to realize she
had entered a world of darkness from which
she would never emerge. My wife varied between cursing fate and accepting God's will for

this curse which showed his love for us, or some such nonsense.

I remember the morning of the 9th all the more because the previous day had been one of great delight for me. I took Marie Thérèse to the Royal Bestiary that afternoon, the 8th, and she was enchanted with the monkey, beguiled by the cockatoos and parakeets. She showed little fascination with the lion as he paced up and down until his food arrived. Then he began a roaring and moaning, which turned into horrible snarling and gluttony as he was thrown hunks of raw meat. For some reason this display made my daughter hysterical, until I thought I was holding a miniature of my wife. Nothing I could say or do hushed her, and to my embarrassment, we became as much a sight for the onlookers as the lion. None of this did I share with the great Dr. M., for if his miracles are true they can proceed without prying into privacies.

But, you may ask (as indeed I now ask myself), why I wrote (unsolicited, mark you) the glorious story of my daughter's recovery as accomplished by the great doctor. I was as much under his magic as she, and he spoke through me to achieve his ends, while I thought I was my own master. It was her general condition that misled me, for she looked better than I had ever seen her: her face clear and bright, her figure shapely, her bosom promising, and her ankle neat. I had produced an excellent young woman notwithstanding her defect. The recovery of her sight led me into transports, for I looked forward to her graceful entry into the courts of Europe, playing like an angel, and for that reason I was always polite to Mozart (and as best I could to his son), who has influence and knows his way around many a court. Imagine my distress as my daughter advanced to her physical perfection (and for this I am grateful to M., for you must give even the devil his due) and her mind became that of a child, indeed such a child as she had never been, for never was she so foolish and silly, helpless in what I soon saw were the confusions engendered by his evil genius. She seemed not to know where she was. She developed a distaste for her mother, and even showed a reluctance to discuss her feelings with me. All the while praising her magic doctor as if the sun, moon, and stars shone through his eyes, as indeed he claimed they did. And of her piano playing, what is there to say?

Up to this, I had overlooked everything in my naïve joy at her "cure." My wife and I could not contain ourselves. We spread the news of the "miracle" far and wide, at court, among our friends, even to her pestilential country cousins who used it as an excuse to come stay with us for a few days (I would not allow them to visit my daughter since half of Vienna was making her into a sideshow). My wife was intoxicated with that charlatan, following him around like a dog as if he were the Emperor himself. Such was the sensation that there was always someone at M.'s door to prove the miracle to himself. Many of these fools had their own little tests with which to satisfy themselves and bring the news back to the world. M. allowed all this, no matter what the strain to my daughter, and I have no doubt it contributed to her confusion. How would you fare with strangers holding up their stupid fingers in front of your eyes and asking you to name their number? I entreated the President of the medical faculty to come and witness. Eventually he agreed and came with a train of his kind. All conducted their examinations to their satisfaction and declared Marie Thérèse cured. My joy was unconfined, and I immediately spent the next three nights putting pen to paper to give an account of what I then believed to be a miracle. I was not alone in my delusion.

Dr. Stoerk himself shared it. It was he, on the kind advice of the Empress, who had treated my daughter for years and who had told us that there was nothing wrong with her eyes, beyond that she was blind, a comment he made with great sagacity, but which, when I repeated it to M. at our first interview, he said was a fine comment and a just one. So much for doctors. And so much for the tortures Stoerk put her under, with his purging and blistering, those damned leeches hanging from her cheeks like black tears which, when my wife first saw, she fainted from the thought that the eyes themselves were trickling down my poor daughter's face. What we have been through!

And in the midst of this, talk of war! As if there were not enough to torment us. Joseph, who, if truth be told, is a shadow of his father, wants to risk war with Prussia. He admires Frederick so much that I can understand his need to destroy him. But the gracious Empress, by whose sagacity we all live in peace, will have something to say about that. They are distant again, so I ferry back and forth with what news of each other they require. Von Kaunitz, of course, passes me without a word, lofty as ever. I have tried to suggest to Her

Majesty that he may have her son's interests more at heart than her own, but to this she only smiles and bids me take another letter, usually to that high-spirited French daughter who is so unlike her mother—given to that foolish Bourbon in a marriage I have heard called that of a nose to a chin (the Hapsburg chin to the Bourbon nose). Perhaps their children will balance their features better. As to Joseph, these days he is as odd as his French sister, who, rumor has it, plays at being a milkmaid when the fancy takes her, dressing up and pretending to be her own subject.

Joseph, Emperor though he is, has lately followed her example by forsaking the trappings of his majesty so as to appear more like his subjects. The other day, when I saw him poring over those maps of his, as if Europe were some pie to be divided at his table, he was so poorly attired that he looked like his own lackey. He has taken up this notion that he must narrow the distance between himself and his subjects by dressing down to them. So disguised, he thinks they will think better of him, and share their thoughts more freely. The opposite is true, for when he joins a group he sometimes goes momentarily unrecognized, so that the courtiers are surprised and assume

their formal manners with a sense of betrayal.
By forsaking his status in this manner, they
are made uncertain of theirs. Some idiots have
even dressed down likewise to suit his conceit,
and if this persists we shall all end up dressed
like our servants who will have no alternative
but to go about in a state of nature. A king
should dress like a king. It is part of his office,
at one with his royalty. Each man shines more
securely in his own setting, and God in his
wisdom has made it so. Confusions of status
should not add to our troubles. We have
enough to trouble us already. How long His
Imperial Majesty, Joseph the Second, son of
the Empress Marie Thérèse, Archduchess of
Austria and Queen of Hungary, shall dress like
his valet's valet is known only to him. For the
rest of us, we pay him the respects due his
blood, not his clothes, and it would be a hu-
morless man indeed who did not lend an ear
to the jokes that have made the rounds, the
usual mouths to the usual ears, followed by
the swish of bows as he appears, pretending
to be less than the rest of us. But as I have
said many times, by some inverse law of social
mathematics, he increases the distance between us by trying to remove it. His brother
Leopold is one who knows how to rule, and if

Joseph keeps this up, I'd as much favor being
in Tuscany, though in Tuscany I would have
to suffer those Italian courtiers who think they
can give us lessons in manners. They are not
as bad as the French, who would take a whole
year to instruct you on how to produce a hand-
kerchief and consider this more important than
a battle. Perhaps as my friend Schlitter suggested when we were waiting for His Majesty
(who has no idea of time but his own), his new
dress of old clothes is to appeal to the peasants
with whom he wants to stock the land—and
not only that, he intends to give it to them, to
the disadvantage of our nobles for whom that
land is as much a birthright as their blood.

His mother, who also favors this, has already
made so many rapid changes within and without that nothing seems certain. Her latest notion is to abolish interrogation of our enemies
and their spies. No more torture! Those who
disobey will have to be punished without the
necessary rack. Do we now coddle those spies
and assassins who go about wearing the masks
of decent folk? Who knows what will result
when no punishment is allowed? There will
be more spies than honest men. It will become
a profession like the law or the Church. Next
she will want to treat our enemies better than

ourselves. Kind as she is, and knowing the many favors she has bestowed on me, I must doubt her wisdom in several domestic matters. I have not uttered a whisper of this to those who solicit my opinion lest I lose her favor, for in her favor lies my daughter's future.

Her interest in my Marie Thérèse, who is named after Her Majesty, has borne fruit in a pension to ease my daughter's affliction and to encourage her pursuit of her music. For it takes her time to learn a new work, and I do not have the time to pick it out for her note by note while she sets it in her memory. Now she has the benefit of the Queen's music master. You can sympathize with my distress, then, when I saw Dr. M. turn my daughter's life into a travesty and her music into discord.

This disaster was masked by her "improvement," if light hurting her eyes can be called improvement, if sudden gusts of tears are improvement, if passion for the great Dr. M. to the neglect of her parents can be called improvement, if baby ways are better than an adult's, if everyone's enthusiasm means that she is improved. *Improved, improved*—everyone used the word until I was sick of it. See how she is improved? Don't you think she is improved? What improvement she has shown! There is much improvement from yesterday. Tomorrow we can expect more improvement. Her general condition is much improved, her color, her figure, her spirits, her sight, her recognition of objects, her happiness, her this, her that—all have improved, and not only improved, but improved beyond measure, beyond expectation, beyond our best predictions, so beyond that the improvement is beyond beyond, improved beyond improvement. And in the midst of all this, I noticed her hands becoming strangers to each other, bumping like two blind puppies.

This is a subtle matter to those of us who care about music. As long as my daughter could play, I knew she had her wits about her, that her mind was not deeply disturbed by the hocus-pocus and that the atmosphere of "miracles" would not greatly harm her. For music was and is the center of her existence, and if she could play, that existence was not in doubt. Listening to her play, as I often did when I stole in unbeknownst to the doctor and his tribe (one of his servants was pleased at the few thalers I gave him for his sick child, if there was a sick child), I heard an odd slippage, as if the tempos were wavering, which for a brief moment I thought was a new idea in the music.

It took me some time to recognize that the hands were not in unison, or rather harmony. The left hand lagged behind the right, and the right sometimes went its own way while the left tried to catch up with it, or so it seemed to me.

But this was only the beginning. For she would break into the middle of her playing with abrupt silences, lifting her hands from the keys and looking at them with that sideways look which she gave to close things, as if they had become objects of puzzlement. Often she did not know that I was present, for I developed a habit of staying behind the curtain near the door (where M. would not see me if he happened upon us). I wished to have the evidence of my own eyes, without prejudice, for announcing myself would often cause her to develop further confusions and stop playing. She began to leave her left hand in her lap and play the treble only, and that she did well. Then she would play the base with her left, disregarding the right. But when she put the two together, with her head almost down to the keys, the music would stay together for a while and then the hands would begin to lose their common sense of each other. At which point she would beat her hands against each other and begin to shake her head, and then her whole body.

This got worse. She wept and made odd noises, not the least like speech, and transferring her displeasure to the piano would beat it with her fists. Her abuse of the piano, combined with strange cries and grunts, was not a happy sight for a loving father. But my good offices, when I approached her, were rudely spurned, and she turned on me like an animal. Imagine my annoyance when M. and his assistants rushed in and attributed her distemper to my intervention! M. had the effrontery to ask me what was I doing here! I told him, with dignity, that I was visiting my own daughter and that if this did not suit His Majesty, I would take her home where I could visit her with impunity. What was more disturbing was the way my daughter, crouching in that charlatan's arms, looked at me (if she could see me) as if I were a total stranger. As I stood there, two of M.'s so-called assistants took up a position on either side of me, standing in their dark skin-tight suits with their arms folded, in a manner apparently passive but to anyone with half a head, menacing as could be. I left with dignity, but not before I addressed

M. with the greatest seriousness and informed
him that I would not delay my return.

So distressed was I that I ignored my carriage. Letting the driver follow me at a distance, I walked home in a fury. During that
walk I decided there was to be an end to this
nonsense. My daughter would return to us as
soon as I could convince all misguided folk that
the treatment was a farce and that my daughter's health and future were being injured by
this madman. It burst on me suddenly, as it
occasionally does at such times, that the eyes
that had been blinded were not my daughter's
but my own. For with all the talk of improvement, with those trivial little litanies of progress ("Today she did this and today she did
that . . .") I had neglected the evidence of my
eyes. Despite the evidence, everyone's enthusiasm had borne me along so that I too
believed her to be cured. Now I know that M.
could make you believe that black was white.
But once my mind had corrected itself, the
evidence overwhelmed me. Persuaded by my
wife's endless whining, and by her uncle, the
Baron, I had allowed myself to neglect my
responsibilities. How painful this was for me.
I paused at our gate. Within the house, my

wife was waiting for news of my daughter. She and her uncle were aligned against me. To them, the great charlatan was a saint, as familiar with the next world as I was with the court, and more influential in his sphere than I in mine.

My problems multiplied. And with them, my outrage. I wanted to reclaim my only child, as was my right. My thoughts were guided only by her welfare. Yet I was forced to scheme like a criminal to have returned to me what was mine by nature. My own haste and generosity had deceived me; my description of my daughter's "cure" was now in everyone's hands. Dr. Stoerk had himself confirmed it. Several had gone to M.'s and seen it with their own eyes. The Empress had heard of it from myself, from the good Schlitter, and several others, and wanted me to present the "cure" at court, complete with a recital. I had been advanced in her favors by this prospect, and even Von Kaunitz nodded to me as we passed in the great hall. The Emperor, of course, notices nothing but his maps, and if his mother shows interest in something it is cause for him to ignore it.

M. himself was on everyone's tongue; his "cures" were yesterday's miracles and today's gossip. Stoerk I cannot touch; he was M.'s master, though there is but a few years between them. The Empress listens to him in all matters pertaining to health and welfare, including her own (along with no torture, we are all to become unbearably healthy). I cannot go to the Baron; his affection is for my wife and not for me. Also he thinks M. a genius and my daughter privileged to be in his care. Nothing will change his mind about the "cure."

Where am I to go? There is Schlitter, of course, who is one of those good fellows always in attendance but never in favor. But then, he is never out of favor either. He is our Chinese wallpaper, a familiar and reassuring background that looks interesting. In the foreground of attention he does not prosper. I once saw the Empress turn to him when no one else was near, and his sober tact in responding to her was to my mind prideful and unbecoming to a courtier. He offers everyone the same courtesy, and this does not suffice for an Empress, or indeed any of our masters whose whim may injure us. He treats everyone, high and low, the same, which he may have learned in France from some of those gentry who seem eager to betray their own kind. The next time he was positioned favorably to respond to her wishes, the Empress ignored him in favor of another. Schlitter doesn't understand that half our employment is to anticipate the royal wishes, and the other half to fulfill them, no matter how odd.

The Empress once asked me to fetch a monkey, for what purpose who can tell, but I went and argued the keeper out of the beast, and carried it back, by which time she had forgotten what she needed it for, and devised for it some other use that served the moment. Poor Schlitter would have asked her for what purpose she needed it, so that he might explain it to the keeper, thereby being advised on how best to fulfill the Empress's wishes for the animal. Then he would probably have brought the keeper back with him to supervise the beast, thereby losing the authority of being the expert of the moment, as well as having no one to blame if things went wrong. But the Empress likes to have him around for no more reason than he is very handsome, but this advantage he does not put to use, either with the Empress or even with the married ladies that approach him. If everyone were like him, these ladies would always be "in-waiting." His good looks seem to force on him a seriousness he is unable to avoid, as if they had put him at a disadvantage. You always have a slight irritation at what he might be if his spirit matched his looks. His wife is plain and jolly.

He is my good friend for no reason that I can fathom. He will never be much advanced in favor, mainly because he wishes to have reasons for every action, and it is the royal prerogative to offer none. Thus he often comes off as forward, even though he has a good command of the courtier's address—as good as any of us. But how ill his questions become a courtier even when phrased as we must: "May it please Your Majesty, with all respect and devotion, for the purpose of serving Your Majesty with all dispatch and care, may I humbly, and in your service, inquire as to the direction of your wishes, that I may enhance my poor service the better to fit your royal command and desire, your humble servant . . ." with a low bow.

All very well, but it puts Her Majesty at *his* service. She much prefers to have a mistake made so that she can raise a finger and shake her head royally, sending you back again to do whatever it was she asked, unclear though it may have been. We work through trial and error, not through precise command. Precision of understanding is for Von Kaunitz and politics, not for us folk who keep things going from day to day—and which, I ask you, is the more essential? To my mind, one is as important as the other, and who can walk around all the time like Von Kaunitz and his like with faces full of portents and a step weighed with *gravitas*?

But none of this helped me fulfill my duty to my daughter, though it did prompt me to solicit Schlitter's advice, so that I went on to his house rather than into my own. He is a good fellow and does not pass on everything he hears. I have never heard back anything I have shared with him. How rare that is in this porous court of ours! Nobody can keep anything to himself, least of all in Paris if one is to judge by the letters from Her Majesty's Bourbonized daughter. Schlitter's advice was predictable: "Have another doctor in Her Majesty's favor visit M.'s establishment and confirm a cure or the lack of one; if confirmed, remove Marie Thérèse since there is no further need of treatment, and if there is a negative report, remove her for that reason." Logical and easily said. "But first," he said, looking at me with a slight embarrassment that told me my wife's tempers were known to more than her husband, "you must convince your good wife that your daughter's interests are best served by this course." I responded that I was not fully in possession of his meaning. He did not reply but looked out the window.

This advice, like that you often receive from disinterested parties, was watertight in theory but full of holes in practice. M. would never give up his prize patient with whom he hopes to convert the world to his magic water and spinning planets. But Schlitter had a good point. He mentioned another doctor. There is no more easily influenced profession in the world, since its jealousies are notorious and we have much amusement at court praising one physician to the other and watching the response. They have their own little court with its favor and influence. But where could I find a doctor who would support my cause? Schlitter and I got to talking about doctors and their virtues, habits and peculiarities, and it came out that his doctor, a fellow by the name of Altdorfer, knew of one Ingenhousz who might be useful to my purpose. Ingenhousz, according to Schlitter's doctor, resented M.'s success and continually spoke against him.

I met with this Ingenhousz at his home, a cavernous place on Elizabetstrasse, with

rooms as dark and formal as Ingenhousz's manners. He had a spade beard and dark eyebrows
out of a paintbrush, so that his face said "doctor" loudly, and when I heard children cry in
the back of the house as I was leaving, my
fancy was that he took off his face when he
returned to these quarters to beget them. This
façade is not uncommon among professional
men, who tend to adjust their looks to the
dignity of their profession so that one feels one
is meeting a diploma rather than a person. This
Ingenhousz, however, was in a fever about M.
You need not doubt me when I tell you that
we spent a pleasant hour tossing his name
around like a shuttle, each of us outdoing the
other in heaping infamy on it. What a pleasure
it was for me to find someone who was not
deceived by this monster, who could quote
chapter and verse on M.'s wretched ministrations and the perversities of his establishment.

Ingenhousz was particularly exercised about
a child called Franzl, whom he said M. had
destroyed. He ranted about the falsities of M.'s
claims, his seduction of innocent girls, his outrageous theories that would set medical progress back a hundred years, all spoken in a deep
voice as black as his beard and eyebrows. It
was good to hear all this, but as I listened, my

mind was at work as to how I might turn his distemper to my advantage. There was little use to be made of Ingenhousz as a witness; his word had to go forth without his person, which was extremely unappealing. His confidence in me increasing—our opposition to M. was a strong mutuality—he spoke of other doctors and their attitudes. He criticized Stoerk, the head of the faculty of medicine, and his staff, who had officially confirmed my daughter's cure. At least, he said, Barth wasn't so deceived.

I knew of Barth. My daughter had complained to me about the confusion he had caused her with his examination. But since several of her visitors had tested her sight in a way that offended her, I had not paid much attention. I did so now. Dr. Barth was well thought of by his fellow doctors—indeed, said Ingenhousz sonorously, he is a pillar of our profession. I had seen him a few times, and pillar indeed he was, as tall and thin as a column with a bent capital, his head always down and tilted in that grave, semi-listening pose that some doctors affect. On further inquiry, I found out that Stoerk thought well enough of him, and Stoerk was the man I had to enlist. He had the Empress's ear. You may ask why

I did not speak directly to the Empress herself. That would have been a serious mistake. How would I explain my previous enthusiasm? My change would appear whimsical, and while courtiers attend to whims, they cannot afford to entertain their own. Also, she would ask Stoerk, and Stoerk, having recently commended M.'s cure, would dismiss my concern as a father's over-solicitousness. And M.'s "cures" had gathered as much support as criticism. Since he was the subject of endless gossip, my complaint would be absorbed in that general fog. To the ignorant I would appear changeable and erratic. No, the best source in such matters is not oneself but a third party, the right third party. I had to get Stoerk to change his mind about Mesmer and to think that change was entirely his own idea. He would speak to the Empress. She would speak to me. I would sorrowfully allow that Stoerk was correct. She would speak to Stoerk again. He would instruct M. to release my daughter back to my keeping, and this nonsense would be at an end.

But how to do it? My plan was to find Barth and have him speak not directly to Stoerk, but at the next doctors' gathering when they meet each month to discuss the world's ills. If Barth could attack M. on grounds that would exercise all his colleagues, their displeasure must influence Stoerk. Barth could hold forth on how M.'s airy methods and phantom successes insult the classic methods (to me they appear barbarous—leeches and purgatives to balance vague humors and distempers) and mislead patients who, when disease proves tenacious, murmur about the painless ministrations of Dr. M. For Stoerk believes above all in the dignity of his profession, and we will see (I get ahead of myself) how long he lets his former friendship with M. weigh against the opinion of his colleagues.

In my view, every man is a hero until his bravery threatens his own interests. Then he does not cut so fine a figure. It is essential when engaged in courses such as this to study each man's vulnerabilities. It is there that his true interests lurk unnoticed. Nor should one neglect the strong points. Take Schlitter, for instance. He is so honorable you can play him like a flute, for you know beforehand how his honor will respond. I will get Schlitter to speak to Barth of my distress over my daughter's "cure," while repeating my praises of M. for his good intentions. This will make Schlitter comfortable, since he won't speak ill of anyone.

He will present my case to Barth as that of a
troubled father, with no whisper of criticism
of that accursed M. Thus will my point be
strengthened, for it will allow Barth to deliver
himself of his violent opinions on M. How hazardous these matters are, for you can never be
sure that they will proceed to the desired end.
If you do not give too many instructions but
allow the instrument of your choice to mold
the general intention through his own partic-
ulars, you will have a better chance of suiting
circumstances to your aims. What measures
we are forced to undertake for the good of
our nearest and dearest! My anger during this
time was never far from the surface. It boiled
slowly inside me, all the more so since I could
not show it, and it burst out in a manner
totally unexpected to myself and, I presume,
to others.

I could not stay away from M.'s house. In
there, behind that high window on the second
floor, my daughter was being coaxed out of her
once fruitful darkness, a darkness no longer
illuminated by her music, which was now one
vast discord. At twilight—the days were getting longer—I skulked like a criminal among
the giant oaks opposite his door, while my
daughter, with the approval of my wife and

her uncle, was being further tortured within by that damned M. Sometimes a figure would appear at the window and my heart would quicken, for I saw every female figure as Marie Thérèse and every male as M. So when a figure appeared, my emotions were immediately switched to one or the other extreme.

I had forbidden my wife to visit M.'s, for I was trying to impair her support of him. My charge, however, seemed to have the opposite effect, for she wailed and moaned about how saintly that damned M. was, "how pure a spirit, how unparalleled—" "A rascal!" I would break in, and the argument would proceed to its usual end, with her in her room, vapors and smelling salts and fainting fits all contributing to her little theater before her audience of servants, whose tongues I'm sure are not still on their days off. That woman wants to paint me as a monster, and herself as a suffering angel. She mistakes the monster. He is in there, weaving spells over her daughter. But she will have none of it. I keep talking about the music, the music. That, my instincts tell me, is the point to advance with her. But she has a way of making me forget my good sense so that I return her abuse, thereby losing my point.

Imagine my surprise, as I lurked among the oaks on the other side of the street, when there I saw my lady bustling along to M.'s, looking behind her as if pursued by robbers and huddling against M.'s door after her knock—attended, mark you, by two of our servants. How this galled me! Mother and father hiding and fleeing, concealing their persons from each other, all for the purpose of reclaiming their daughter—or at least that is my aim; my wife's aims are known to her, for her brain is always addled and its odd logic issues from confusion. She disappeared within and I found myself at M.'s door wondering how I got there. The blank door seemed to insult me, making me half mad with temper.

How time passes when one is furious is a mystery. I may have been at that door five minutes or five seconds. All I know is that with each moment my anger mounted upon itself and demanded action. This rush is familiar to me, and Schlitter had often counseled me to moderate my sudden bursts. More than once he had nodded approvingly as I have grown red on the face suppressing some insult or stupidity, until his nods so added to my distemper that I vented my anger on him, who is, after all, trying to help me. Schlitter should take

Holy Orders, he is so temperate. I heard a great hubbub inside and recognized—I would recognize them anywhere—my wife's screams, which have a disastrous character, as if the world were coming to an end and needed an audience to bring it off properly. I drew back to thunder on the door with my stick—bedamn the bell—when it suddenly opened and I found myself embracing one of my wife's servants fleeing the house in a panic. His eyes became saucers when he saw me, for he was on his way to fetch me and the premature fulfillment of his mission left him speechless. I hurled him aside and ran towards the bedlam where I fancied my wife the victim of some calamity, and as for my daughter's fate, God knows.

In this emergency, I threw aside my cane, and, fearful of those muscular fellows in their dark skin-suits, I placed my hand on my sword—a rapier, more for decoration—to prepare myself for the worst. What a sight I saw! My daughter tossed on the floor like a milliner's bundle, my wife lying half on top of M. with her bonnet awry and her bodice burst open while she pounded on his face and chest. Two of those fellows pulled her away but she broke free and rushed over to my daughter

who had begun to gather herself and was almost risen (I glimpsed her eyes wide-open
with a look of complete blindness) when my
wife half-embraced her and then, to my horror, hurled her against the wall where she
collapsed into another bundle. The room suddenly seemed occupied by a multitude, for
there was no clear path to my wife, who was
now on the floor again, screaming away, or to
my daughter, who was my first concern. As I
pushed towards my daughter I bumped into
M. It seemed that my sword, which I had quite
forgotten, was still in my hand, for M. shouted,
"The sword! the sword!" In an instant, another
set of those fellows fell upon me and forced
me down. So there lay the entire Paradies family, all on M.'s floor, one dead to the world,
one screaming as if judgment day had come,
and myself looking at the world upside down,
for they had bent me back over a hassock, with
my throat higher than my chin so that I could
hardly breathe. With a heavy hand on my forehead, another holding my sword hand, and
another on my chest, I could not speak. All
this visited on the person and family of a secretary to the Empress! And in front of servants!

While I was thus incapacitated, M., holding
my daughter's head in his lap and in no way

allaying my anxieties about her, spoke to me as I have not been spoken to since a schoolboy before whipping. As if all this abuse were my family's just deserts! Not only that, but he did not allow me to recover my dignity and respond. His fellows righted me up and marched me to the door. Looking back, I saw my wife and daughter being attended to. My wife's hysterics declined from opera to quiet sobbing, a preface to her recovering whatever sense she has. My daughter was carried to the couch and laid upon it, carefully, I will admit. M. approached, brushing off his wretched robe with planets and signs on it, and told me icily that he could not answer for my daughter's future, that her health was now at risk as a result of our behavior, and that he would continue with my daughter as long as I never set foot in his house again. I heard this as in a dream, for my passion had spent itself. In the blink of an eye, I was outside again, staring at M.'s front door, this time in the company of one of my servants.

The door again infuriated me with its blankness. Before, I had not known what lay behind it. Now I had that knowledge. I did not know which was worse. My servant bowed to me as if nothing had happened and had the insolence to touch my shoulder and indicate the street.

I fetched him such a clout as he will not easily forget and told him to take himself off, which he did to the far side of the street. I last saw him half-hidden by the trees as I set off at such a pace that I was panting in no time. As my mind rehearsed what had transpired, my discomfort turned into a rage that shortened my breath further. I switched at mid-pace and headed for Schlitter's house. He was in and received me with the distant thoughtfulness that is his pose at court.

For some reason this irritated me further, and I reproached him for lack of sympathy for my daughter's plight. He calmed me so that I was able to discharge some of my anger and relate the story of M.'s perfidious insults to my family and my person. "This," he said judiciously, "has gone too far. I will have a word with Stoerk." Seeing some movement in his position, I calmed myself further to take advantage of it.

"I do not wish," I said, "to cause a general discomfort, which would reach the Empress's ears. For all his infamy, Mesmer believes his nonsense. He is his own best follower, and I wish him no harm and seek only my daughter's well-being. It may be that she has reached the limit of what benefits his treatments can provide. But what is the use of sight if it itself becomes an affliction that deprives my daughter of all her skills: her cardplaying, her lace-making, her music? How is a parent to think of someone who has so altered his daughter's affections that she sees her father as an obstacle to her health, a father who, after eighteen years of nurturing, suddenly becomes a stranger to her hopes and desires? My dream is to see her playing again before the Empress with friends and courtiers assembled, the applause nourishing her desire to beguile and enchant the great capitals of Europe, to make a circlet of cities into a crown—"

Schlitter held up his hand, and, having the advantage of me—I now noticed that my clothes were considerably disordered—concluded the conversation, assuring me, as his servant saw me out, that all would be well if I had patience. Patience, patience indeed. Had I not already had enough patience to outlast the foundations of this house? But patience was what I needed now, to let events proceed in conformity with my purpose, not to interfere or guide, but to trust providence, which is not my nature. All I could do was listen and listen with as many ears as were available to me, through the court, through Schlitter as far as he would speak, and through Barth and his medical friends, while I adopted a posture of one who forbears and suffers nobly.

As is the way of these things, the signs were obscure and elusive—odd whispers, a look, a silence—for there is as much at such times to misread as read. I aided matters as much as was judicious, visiting Ingenhousz again for some advice on a supposed twitch of an eye, which I mimicked as best I could while he examined me, after which it took but little time to sound out his thoughts on M. and to provide him with what ammunition I could. When I saw Schlitter at court (in truth, we rarely visit each other at home) he had, as I expected, little to say beyond a meaningful nod which indicated, as much as a finger on the lips, that my daughter's trials were not a subject for conversation but that they were being attended to.

My wife, long recovered and sulking at home, was of no account, for she varied between anger at our daughter, anger at the servants, some of whom finally left, and anger at me. Only a saint would have refrained from chastising her following our debacle at M.'s, which went around the city. God knows there were enough witnesses present from the *beau monde*, from the servant class, and as full a complement of dupes and fools as you could find to carry tales. And go round the tales did. At court, Samovitch, that damned Russian, asked me solicitously if my wife had recovered. Those who had put him up to it turned blank faces when I turned on them. I responded that I had not known that my wife was indisposed and would consult him in future to find out the state of my family's health whenever such a need arose. He looked mystified since his German is not subtle.

I kept an account of those who tormented me in this glancing way. These accounts must always be paid off slowly, for to pay them off without waiting for the proper opportunity is to return the negative to oneself rather than to your object. The Empress is a master of such subtleties, for she notices things that many of us miss, and seems to know the state of affairs among us underlings better than we do ourselves. For instance, a few days after this incident with Samovitch, she asked me, innocently, "What has your Russian friend to say about St. Petersburg these days?" with her usual smile, into which one can read a thousand meanings, depending on the occasion. She always knows more than she pretends. The Emperor is so taken up with himself and his affairs that, except for Von Kaunitz, he notices nothing about the intrigues of his immediate circle. I swear Frederick and Catherine are more substantial to him than his wife. He is like one who looks always at the distance and never sees his feet, contemplating grand schemes but ignorant of the first practical steps.

It is through the Empress that I can damage others, though her sense of fairness is an obstacle. She is only unfair when an inference is made about her person; about politics, she will listen and argue (she argues powerfully). She has grown so in circumference that her movements are quite restricted, and at any reference to this, no matter how obscure or guarded, she loses her habitual sweetness of expression. We must treat her as if she were a supple young maiden. I paid off Waldheimer when he was arranging the Empress's annual pic-nic, to be held this year on his estate. He was going about it with much formality and self-importance. I allowed to the Empress, at a private moment when taking a letter, that Waldheimer was worried about her transport and that he could not make as much use of the scenic aspect of his grounds as he had hoped, since the party must stay close to the mansion.

I bent my head and there was a pause before she resumed her letter. The pic-nic was canceled, not the next day, but the day after, and Waldheimer was walking around crestfallen, making excuses about the uncertainty of the weather, though the pic-nic was two weeks distant.

At what moment does something change? I had thought myself alone in my efforts to recover my daughter. But while M. has his enemies, as I have mine (which of us does not?), they had not perceived my case as one by which they could injure M. At one moment I felt myself pushing back the tide; the next moment I seemed to have allies—and I cannot tell you when that moment was. It was not just the support of Barth and Ingenhousz, or even Schlitter. Theirs I knew I had. But others, through a nod or a more favorable greeting, or even a sympathetic inquiry about my daughter's health, gave me certainty that matters were ripening for me. My opportunity to speak to the Empress arose when she was lamenting all her daughters' lack of sense, particularly her French daughter, who lost her head over trifles and was indifferent to large matters.

I presumed to agree so meaningfully that she amiably suggested my daughter play for her soon. "Was she not to play for me last week?" she added. "Alas," I said, "she can no longer play." At which the Empress expressed surprise. "I am not allowed to see her," I said, "while the good Dr. Mesmer carries out his plans." "We thought," said the Empress, "that her affliction had been cured." "Your Majesty," I said, "she is worse. She can no longer see or play. But the good doctor feels he can benefit her still. Who knows that he may be right? But my wife and I miss her sorely. Her music is silent and we are much concerned. I do not wish in any way to cause Your Majesty concern over her person. Your Majesty has always favored her beyond her gifts and station, and if my weakness as a father brings tears to my eyes, I have these many weeks concealed my feelings from you who have shown her so much favor and have so little time even for large matters. I am helpless. The good doctor is firm. I must not see her. And while I have the highest regard for the good doctor, I am tormented by those rumors—I'm sure groundless—which issue from his salon."

"What rumors?" said the Empress.

"I should not have spoken," I answered reluctantly, "for all the world is made up of rumors, most of them false. I worry not just for my daughter, who is, I'm sure, as safe as in my own home, but for other young girls in that strange place of magic. I'm sure Your Majesty, to whom nothing is hidden, has heard about strong young men who bear them off to padded rooms to suppress their crises, which the good doctor feels is a part of their cure. But, Your Majesty, that is the way the timid mind works when one has a daughter and knows something of the world. Without the opportunity to set my fears at rest—for the good doctor is adamant about closing the door on my wife and myself while he pursues his cure—such fears find ground to flourish. Am I doing the best for my daughter? That is the question of every parent to himself."

"Have you spoken to Stoerk?" said the Empress.

"I know him but slightly, Your Majesty. I do know that he and Mesmer are friends. He was one of Mesmer's examiners, though they are close in age. He visited Mesmer and examined my daughter, your namesake. But I have taken too much of your time, and Your Majesty's gracious interest is far in excess of . . ." I could not finish the sentence because I could not find a good end for it, but the Empress mistook my pause as evidence of deep emotion. She said decisively, "I am glad to know of this," and, resettling her posture to indicate the conversation was over, returned to the letter.

I contained my exhilaration until I had bowed my way out. Would she speak to Stoerk herself or have someone else do it? If she herself did so, Stoerk would have no latitude in his response. I knew that Stoerk was under pressure from the medical faculty. Though he considered himself a friend of Mesmer's, or at least more friend than not, he could not withstand the Empress's word on the one hand and the irritations that Barth, Ingenhousz, and others provided on the other. He might find it prudent to suggest to M. that he release my daughter, for no man's honor is above what threatens his interests. This would be painful for him, for Stoerk parades his honor like a cockade, and being very tall, is able to look down on all of us. As a compromise, for I do not wish Stoerk's ill will (he is close to the Empress), my daughter might visit M. each day and return to us in the evenings, missing a day now and then until the whole affair trailed off.

About this time, being exasperated with inaction, I spoke to Von Semper, a dull fellow who is the Archbishop's brother-in-law, and solicited his opinion on the rumors of the mischief M. practiced on young women, and how such stories must irritate and concern His Grace. Von Semper, who is taciturn, merely grunted, but I feel he took my point, for he is blessed with four young daughters and no son. Hopeless though it probably was, I had my wife visit her uncle, Baron de Colnbach, and so well instructed her in what to say that she wept several times prior to her departure at the misery of our plight. Whether she passed on my point accurately to her uncle I have no way of knowing. Her reports on her experiences are so unreliable that they often seem to have befallen someone else, even for events at which I have been a witness. He received her kindly and she wept, that is as much as I can vouch for. But then, how moving are tears that flow equally for happiness and sorrow, and often without cause? Again, I swallowed my impatience and returned to waiting—most difficult when one has an open and impulsive nature.

A Dr. Ost was waiting for me in the blue waiting room. So said my servant when he opened the door as I returned from a difficult day shuttling between their majesties, for the

Empress had me make a report on the findings of the Committee on Public Morals, but, being in a dark mood, she found nothing but fault in their recommendations and found further fault in the manner of my report, which was just the same as on other occasions when she had complimented me. Even the mention of Leopold's new successes in Tuscany did nothing to relieve her distemper, the cause of which remained obscure to me. There are many contradictions in her and thus many surprises, not that surprises are something new. One of her concerns can appear out of the blue while in the midst of dealing with another, and she is irritated when one cannot follow. Perhaps Mesmer could read her mind on such occasions. Like many rulers, her thoughts run on several levels and my success with her is due to my rapid adjustment to her abrupt changes. Thus there are many matters with which I must be conversant simultaneously, and she takes some pleasure in testing my preparedness by making me jump hither and thither.

These thoughts were occupying my mind as I found myself shaking Dr. Ost's hand, remonstrating with myself for my lack of attention, for when I saw him I recognized him as the Dr. Ost who was made court physician this last year. So I suddenly became all ears and showed him every good manner. I had thought he was someone's relative looking for a favor at court—which I am pleased to grant if it is in my power, depending, of course, on their ability to return it later, for unreturned favors become a weight on one's mind. Ost, who is formal to the point of rudeness, began directly.

"I come to speak of your daughter, sir," he said. "I have visited Dr. Mesmer's clinic and spoken to him and to your daughter. I wish now to speak to you."

I suppressed my emotion and responded: "I am at your service, sir."

"On what basis do you demand her return?"

"I could give you a thousand reasons, sir, but first and last because she is my daughter."

I quickly saw that no expression of emotion, or appeals to his sympathies would further me with Dr. Ost. So I confined myself to a recital of history, her momentary improvement, her subsequent decline, including her most un-daughterly feelings for her parents.

"Her confusion of mind, her altered feelings, the loss of her gifts, her exposure to influences which, according to accounts that I have heard, can tragically mislead her life, which life is already handicapped by misfortune—all of these speak in one voice for the return of her person to these familiar surroundings where her spirit can repair itself in quietness in the bosom of her loving family."

Ost, however, showed not a flicker of a response, but made notes in a small notebook, peering at it through his glasses and then, without expression, looking at me over them.

"Why then, sir," he said, "did you write such an account of Dr. Mesmer's miracle in restoring your daughter's sight? And why, after your last conflict involving your wife, did she write an apology for your behavior and request Dr. Mesmer to continue his treatment?"

"No, sir," I said, "that was an earlier letter and did not refer to the disturbance a week ago. As for my first enthusiasm, which of us does not show gratitude when one thinks one's nearest and dearest is delivered from ill health and misfortune? All the more painful, then, when one's hopes are mocked by their subsequent contradiction."

"Is it true," said Ost, "that your wife on occasion has abused the girl?"

I dropped my face in my hands and was silent. "Dr. Ost," I said after a sufficient pause, "you are a man of the world. Which of us does not have his domestic griefs? My wife, as you know, is the niece of Baron de Colnbach, and the Baron is one of Dr. Mesmer's first supporters. My wife dearly loves him, and she is confused between her responsibilities to her daughter and to her uncle. My wife is under great strain and I fear for her. She is already attending two doctors, both of whom I'm sure are known to you. My daughter's absence has had the most profound effect on her health, and I have now not one but two sources of anxiety."

I was getting more than tired of Dr. Ost. His expression never changed, nor did his posture, stiff as a parcel no part of whose contents must escape its package. His face is like a crab apple with a little beak of a nose. I judged him to be about fifty-five. He is so precise in dress and address that he looks like a caricature of a doctor in a play. He fills his part so well that he is invisible when not employed in the action and predictably present when he is. He looked to me like someone who could go to bed in these clothes and get up in the morning unruffled. I was so irritated with him, and so irritated that my irritation must be dissembled, that my mind began of its own accord to make speculations about his passions, for all of

us have them, you can be sure of that. I was
fancying him stripped like a shrimp and exercised in some obscenity when I remembered
with a shock that he had come to court with a
young and beautiful wife whose décolletage
excited the usual interest from some younger
courtiers who consider themselves rakes, and
who speculated with amusement as to Ost's
capacities to avail himself of such bounty. I
also remember that she had rejected advances
from two of the most practiced seducers,
thereby losing them what they had bet on their
prospects. For this young woman doted on this
stick before me, hung on his arm and gazed
down at him with every evidence of adoration.
My obscene thoughts rehearsed themselves.
What fires were lighted by this fellow with
such kindling available to him every night?

Pursuing my aims with all gravity to his face,
while having him naked in my mind's eye,
leaping back and forth in a hurry to take advantage of his young wife's opulence, I must
have seemed a little distracted. He uttered the
first word of what could, with a little exaggeration, be construed as sympathetic.

"Your case, sir, is delicate. It is my task to
elicit the facts. There is much contradiction

here. There are important forces in operation
with your daughter at their center."

"To what end is your visit, sir?" I responded.
He had come from court. He was investigating
my daughter's case. Did he come from Stoerk?
Was it at the Empress's bidding? I knew nothing of this man's connections and could not
inflect my responses to his interests. Sometimes the obvious is so before us that we cannot
perceive it. I was so in the habit of explaining
my daughter's case to everyone who asked that
I had fallen into that habit with Ost. It slowly
dawned on me that this was the moment, the
opportunity, the very seed of my labors burst-
ing into flower before my eyes. Yet my mind
continued its search. The Empress would
never speak directly. Or would she? Who was
the intermediary between her and Ost, if there
was one? Von Kaunitz? Never! Van Swieten
was too old. Schlitter? What hand had Schlitter
in this? She knows that we are friendly. Ost
interrupted me.

"I will now take my leave." Before every
action, I noticed, he announced his intention
to perform it. I will now go to the door. I will
now get my coat and cape from your servant.
I will now walk through your front door, and

indeed he did, bearing within him that spark of passion that must at some time animate his person to requite that young wife. I watched him go with jealousy and exultation.

How much we imagine when we cannot witness the events that influence our fate! For the next week my fancies invented endless conversations. What had Ost said to Stoerk? What had Stoerk said to the Empress? What had she said to Stoerk? Had Schlitter been asked for his advice? (He raised a restraining hand and shook his head when I asked.) Had he spoken to Barth? Where were Barth and Ingenhousz? What was said at the meeting of the medical faculty? How had Mesmer responded to Ost? What had each and every person said, or not said, what inflection had they used, could I account them friend or foe? All of this so preoccupied me that I became absent from myself, presenting to others a distant air, with a slight smile around the lips (where else?), and a slower gait which I hoped would be taken for gravity and measure. Only with the Empress was I fully present. She did not speak again of my daughter.

I was endlessly aware of the fragility of the exchanges taking place between those who were determining my daughter's fate. For nothing proceeds according to our expectations, and chance and whimsy mock our best plans. Man is a poor instrument, and woman worse. As each talked to the other in my imagination, I had a sense of an intricate and reciprocal mechanism, which, if properly fashioned, would pass my intention through it tick by tick. The image of a little clock formed itself in my thoughts, one of those jeweled fantasies in an egg that the Empress received from her sister-Queen in Russia. And in my fancy, Time, as in an allegory, sat upon the jeweled egg. I have sometimes held the egg on the Empress's mantelpiece in my hand between letters, admiring how it ticked its way to perfection, each unit of its mechanism precise and foreordained. How easily is its perfection injured. One of the dwarfs at court opened another Russian egg and held it to his ear, grinning. His hair became entangled in its machinery. When commanded by the equerry to lay it down, he leaped in fright and the egg, no longer ticking, clung like an opulent bug to his hair. (He was banished to the kitchen thereafter.)

So with my affairs. I fancied that I held the perfect little mechanism of my fortunes to my ear and suffered lest anything interfere. I spoke to no one, possessing my soul in patience as best I could and rebuking my wife for echoing my own anxieties, for she tolerates uncertainty worse than myself, if that is possible. Imagine how shocking it was to me when I went to court a week after Ost's visit to find all my hopes dashed to nothing, my precious egg crushed by a vast machine beyond my imagining.

Von Kaunitz was where I had let my instincts fail me. He had been running back and forth between the Empress and her son. My fellow secretaries had been more than busy. I had noticed this, of course, but not made much of it. I knew what was happening, but in such a way that it was never fully possessed by my understanding. For there are always rumors of war, and the Empress's obsession with Prussia seemed no greater and no less. For all her concern during the seven years of that disastrous war, she did not realize how profoundly it had changed the world. Yet her eyes were always on Prussia, as were those of her firstborn. In this, Joseph was his mother's son. So, in a mix of filial duty (to her wish) and rebellion (by daring what she would not), he launched us into war with Prussia. Or at least, it was imminent.

Such was my state at that moment that my daughter's predicament mattered more to me than the withering of our youth in the field. This gives you some idea of how deeply the wrenching of my only child from my bosom had affected my very being. In all this preparation for war, how far did my anguish cast its shadow? No farther than that of a twig in a forest. I cursed Joseph (to myself), cursed Prussia and all pertaining to Frederick, and cursed the fate that had put the bars of great events around my daughter's imprisonment. My wife and I, joined in our common grief, relieved it with anger and arguments, and though I could not blame my wife for Joseph's desire to conquer Prussia, I managed to find some connections that sufficed for argument, since her uncle, like the Empress, was one of those who had never let Silesia out of his mind.

I partook of these events in one important way. It was I, not Von Kaunitz, who was sent to summon Joseph to his mother's rooms at Schönbrunn, and bowed my way out as he spread his maps on the huge table already thick with them. We all know now how the old lioness bit her cub and put him back in the cage, saving us and all those children who are war's first fodder. However, that is not my story.

My wife and I were sitting silently in the large withdrawing room in the front of the house. We had exhausted all we had to say to each other and our mutual presence was not one of comfort. If we opened a conversation, its course was so clear that to pursue it was to fatigue ourselves on exactly the same circuit, returning us, freshly exhausted, to our distemper.

The great bell rang and after the usual interval of listening and waiting, the footman brought in a sealed envelope on a silver salver that had belonged to my wife's father. That white oblong on the silver tray, picking up the light in the darkness, is an image I will never forget. I opened the envelope. It contained two letters, one to me from a fellow secretary drawing my attention to the second (a copy) which was—my heart leaped and my breath stopped as if my body must arrest itself while my eyes consumed the letter's substance—addressed to Mesmer. The phrases ran through my eyes and half into my comprehension: ". . . put an end to this imposture . . . restore the girl to her loving parents . . . if this can be done without risk." I turned the letter over to find the signature, crushing it (you can see the creases of my impatience, for I have it still) and there, shining like a jewel, was the name "Stoerk"!

"Return!" "Return!" Through the thunder of great events my little mechanism had ticked its way to perfection. What joy! What joy! My daughter, my daughter! I shall have my daughter!

5

dreamed of her last night, and this has disturbed my day. Why should some things return to us in old age, in a form so vivid, that they demand a young man's response from a body no longer capable of such exercise? In my fancy, in my dream, she posed before me, drifting through the darkened room, urgently followed by my desire, in a way totally at variance with the facts. For I never desired her. I was to her a father, and she to me a child by proxy. In my dream, in that distant darkness, I stroked her body to coax the magnetic fluids to circulate to her afflicted eyes, gathering them from limbs and body to bring light to her eyes—for the eyes take up so much energy that in such cases we need all the body's resources. I never disrobed her. I simply reached under her costume, with my own eyes closed, to share her condition, and there stroked gently as was demanded by my therapy. But in my unwanted dream, thirty years later, her bare thighs glimmered in the twilight while I stroked them from inside the knee to the vicinity of her sex, before which, as God is my judge and my wife is my witness, I stopped short. This dream has tortured me, for it is not consistent with my memory, nor with my opinion of myself, and thus has pained me greatly.

I have never had the slightest desire for any of my patients. No doctor would, if he respects his profession, acknowledge—even to himself—such a notion. Between our patients and ourselves is a barrier reinforced by the honor of our profession as practiced through a lifetime. Yet in this dream, with a vividness of

which I am ashamed, my therapeutic strokings
become lustful caresses, and her eyes roll upward under their lids, not with blindness and
terror, but with ecstasy. On awakening, I
found an insurrection at the center of my very
nature; for the first time in two decades, my
member recalled its youth in a way that
seemed as disgusting to me as if I had seen
such a stirring on a dead man on the autopsy
table. And at my advanced year, when I am
preparing myself for my departure!

I feel so unjustly treated by my own mind
that I have been angry for several days, being
short with that new housekeeper and abrupt
with my neighbors. Where does this grotesque revision of my history come from? Why
should my mind betray me in this fashion?
Many of my patients have been of extraordinary beauty, both men and women, and I have
felt no desire for either, beyond the pleasure
one has in whatever is so well-made that it
seems a compliment to Creation. It is also true
that desire has never moved my compass one
fraction away from the intent and goal of my
life, which is—I almost said "was," for apart
from this unsettling disturbance, I sometimes
feel myself dead already and thus better qualified for retrospect—to benefit mankind

through my discoveries. While I speak of the race in general, I cannot honor those individual members who have blocked my way with their ignorance and hatred. But these thoughts of Marie Thérèse have thrown my waking mind into such confusion that I hesitate to go to sleep (and sleep was always for me a voyage of solace and delight) lest thoughts of her again appear to disturb me. So between my waking and sleeping minds there is much mistrust, and my meditations on my life, which are necessary to me at this time, are interrupted and confused. I hope this dream will not recur. I wish to be free of it to pursue my thoughts in that state of calm reflection which Cicero— whom I have by my bedside—advises us is indispensable to finding meaning in the vicissitudes of our past.

. . .

I have always felt my spirit part of a harmony that has infinite dimension and duration, making of time a vast stillness in which motion is an illusion we are constrained to believe. Here by the lake, as my soul approaches the magnetic sea in which we hereafter have our being, the here and now sometimes becomes a prison in which memory has difficulty inscribing its

window. When the past does not revisit me,
I feel its unseen weight press my future into
a narrow band. At such times, without access
to my past, the present becomes strange to
me, known only through the fits and starts of
my body as it goes about its business of keeping
me alive. I am eighty years old and will die
next year.

This stage of life is thought to be a time when
I remake myself by meditating on the events
that shaped my life. But the pain in my bladder
often distracts me from those retrievals that
the Holy Mother tells us should be part of our
summation before presenting ourselves for
judgment—if judgment there be, which I
doubt, since I have never believed in the extension of the legal profession into the celestial
realm. My mind, of whose workings I have
become so aware that it seems to have doubled
itself, latches on to present distractions more
easily than to past events. Just now, thinking
of the Revolution and the violent fate of several
of those who judged me, I look out the window
at the lake and am startled by a vast monster,
at least fifteen feet long, with webbed wings,
which makes a sudden run on the window-
pane. To be frightened by a fly when thinking
of the guillotine! The reason being, of course,

that I am wearing my half-glasses, and, shifting my glance from this page to the lake, unfocused the monster, until my eye, correcting itself like a miniature telescope, restored the proportions of things.

Beyond the window, the lake is a sheet of light brighter than the pewter-toned sky above it, a sky that looks thick with substance, as if the air were heavy. The lake, along which winds or currents have ruled some long, straight lines, seems as light as air, and this inversion takes my fancy, with the usual conceit that this is perceived only by myself. This sense of aloneness, of being the only one who sees, is familiar to me, not less so now when I have just received a doctor from Berlin, named Wolfart, bringing news of yet another success of my method. But this does not please me particularly, for I am sick of such successes. There seems to be a contrary force in human affairs that keeps the world in a perpetual state of disharmony. Yet with so little time ahead of me, I should not be so cynical. Through all my struggles, I have honored my belief in my system that has improved the lot of thousands and, through my followers, tens of thousands, a system on which I have speculated without fear of my profession in my latest work. What have I to lose now? Whose favor can be withdrawn from me? What hardships can await beyond those that nature has already assigned to me? I have suffered the blight of misunderstanding all my life. I have been betrayed by friends and courted by enemies. My proofs have been discounted, my amiable desires for mankind perverted into avarice by the avaricious. In my old age I have had to sing for my supper, when the banquet once was mine in Vienna (where they put me in jail on my return), and in Paris (they finally returned to me a third of the value of my properties). The Revolution did not improve mankind. The agony through which we all passed has left us better and worse. Yet some good friends remain, pure in spirit and of open mind, their souls unburdened by the darkness that now swaddles Europe, as battles rage and further convulsions await us, the end of which I shall not see.

This does not disturb me. In our youth we feel we are entitled to satisfactory endings. But in our maturity we know there is no end but our own. We always leave before the play is over, and knowing the end doesn't amount to much, one end being as good as another. All around us are endings and beginnings, legions of them, perceived or not by the needs of our own natures. The harmonious world is as far away as when I began my researches; ignorance is a giant stretched across Europe whose stirrings all but crush what we value most. Yet these thoughts are but shadows on the wall behind me. They fade at the sight of the shining ellipse of my plate on the table, my yellow canary taking its position on the rim as it does before each meal cooked by that new woman who does not yet do things to my taste. These thoughts lift from my brain, as the morning vapors over the lake burn slowly away in the heat of the sun; where the mountain's flank meets the water, there is a line of silver light. The lake is still as a mirror, reflecting that massive flank until it is cut off by the near shore, leaving my fancy to imagine the rest of the mountain plunging into the deep, hidden like much of our past life. Shivers of memory pucker the surface, which holds that image of the past in its depths. Poised over our own reflection, we see, in that transparent mirror, surface and depth, present and past in one. The present is so insistent when one's discomforts make each moment a prison from which one longs to escape.

But when the body allows—and how the

body grumbles its way into our consciousness every morning—my animal thoughts run back and forth, exercising themselves on the tread-mill of the present, burrowing into the past, nosing ahead to expectations that always arrive in some disguise or other, for our expectations so blind us that we misperceive what has not yet happened. Indeed, the movements of the past seven years have been an image of my own mind, from Frauenfeld to Constance to Meersburg, where I am finally settled in. This is the end of my journeys, and I draw closer to the beginning of a journey in which I have full confidence but of which I have imperfect knowledge.

I speak of "I," and that notion of myself, as I reflect by the lake, is strange to me, for there are several persons I have met in recent months, all of them myself. In these last years, I am more various than I have ever been. I thank my stars for this gift—and gift it is—of variousness. For it enables some of me to es-cape what is familiar and to spy upon myself. I see my face in the mirror, and smile, since there is a conspiracy between us. That other fellow is more cunning than I, and I have a fancy that he sees my secrets while he keeps his own. He does not flatter me; at times he shows me my vanity, at times (in an unfriendly light) my age; at times he provokes by showing me the radiant visage of my prime. His eyes always anticipate mine—when I try to surprise him, the rascal in the mirror recomposes my features to his own liking before I can spy on him again.

All my several selves are sometimes gathered into one when I wake at night. In part because of my fear that the dream of Marie Thérèse will return, I no longer sleep well, even though the night was always my joy. Then the illusion of light is removed and the heavens revolve in harmony with the turning earth, each motion of which I fancy I feel in my bosom. I awake. And in the darkness— velvet, dense, infinite, as if I myself were a planet adrift—something abruptly returns me to the present. Bodiless in the dark, I hurtle towards an abyss into which I am precipitated over the margin of life. My heart thumps faster and faster, as if it would lock in one continuous spasm. At such moments I am prematurely dead, yet aware that this vision—which is not frequent—is a sign that I still live. Out of such moments are saviors and tyrants born. This vision consoles me in the daylight hours, for it sharpens my thoughts with its solemnity,

while at the same time I dismiss it as yet another convincing illusion. What adventures we
live through between sleep and wake, and
what monsters roam in the image of our own
fears and terrors! And I have seen so much of
terror, when the body social, a city, a country,
and an age shivered with this vision.

Watching my mind run by itself, I smile at
its predictable egotism and follies. So I am in
two minds these days, or, perhaps more truly,
between two minds. One which runs a familiar, if consoling, course and the other, more
alert and watchful, capable of lifting me above
this earthly plane into an area that is not remembrance or sentiment, but, if this were possible, a remembrance of the future; I seem to
see the future very clearly at times in a matter-
of-fact way unacceptable to my scientific colleagues with their noses stuck in logical
grooves. It is very strange, this future, for it
is neither cloudy nor clear, but a kind of potency in which I find myself feeling very alert.
Out of it thoughts arrive by way of images or
feelings or both, which some inner judge immediately rules true or false. These feelings
and images are rejected more often than not.
I think of these as various futures, of which
one will occur, and of which a few are likely.

Sometimes I see their futures when I look at people; it seems to stream out of me in one great exhalation. I sense a feeling they will have, though I do not know what event will provoke it. Occasionally, I can see an event, or image, but do not know its feeling. At times, with great conviction, I see both. When I know it for good or ill, I want to tell them good news or to avoid this or that, but this responsibility confuses me, for I know the future, which is likely, may not happen as I see it; the circumstances that provoke its image in my mind may change and deliver an alternative. I am uncomfortable talking of this, even to myself, for people think there is some witchcraft to it, when it is very matter-of-fact. These visions, if such they be, are, I think, transferred through the universal fluid, which knows not the divisions of time to which we are normally subject.

. . .

So I play my glass harmonica and watch my canary drop a sugar cube in my coffee, and look out the window at the lake where the light changes between one glance and the next. The lake is like a face in which I can read every flicker of expression. Such are the modest de-

lights that arise out of my semi-idleness,
though it looks more like idleness to others
than to myself. For my mind is full of ideas,
memories, speculations, anticipations, and a
desire for knowledge that can yet transform
the lot of every man. From the world outside,
where my ideas run parallel to my own existence, rumors of them come back to me—last
month from Berlin, with Wolfart.

I will die next year, as the gypsy said. I will
die here in Meersburg, for this is my last
move, except for the final one when my spirit
parts from this body which has accommodated
it well. I am convinced the pains I suffer when
voiding are not the usual impediments of old
age, but the symptoms of a lesion in my bladder. My will insists on an autopsy to confirm
a diagnosis in which I will no longer be interested. There is no doubt in my mind that the
gypsy spoke the truth in Paris. I have always
known, since then, that my life had its terminus somewhere in my eighty-first year, before 23rd May 1815. The sense of this end I
have observed within myself with curiosity,
and the observer often seems quite distant
from myself, though of which self this observer
is composed sometimes eludes me. Again I am
returned to the interval between myself and,

for want of a better word, he who observes
me. Why the gypsy made this prophecy, I do
not know. She came, in the mysterious manner
they cultivate, into my baquette room near the
Place Vendôme and, as the fashionable ladies
withdrew from her, presented herself directly
to me. She asked for no alms, no favors, no
treatments for her or hers. In her arms she
carried an infant which, I am told, they often
rent. When she requested my palm, I lent it
to her, since I do not disrespect fortune-
tellers, nor any form of knowledge that can
enlighten us. While the ladies watched, she
studied my palm and said that my life would
be made up of change and much disappointment but that in the future my name would
pass from tongue to tongue in many languages
and would always signify a mysterious power.
There would be indications of this, she said,
before I died, which event would arrive in my
eighty-first year. The ladies listened, some
pretending not to. Some asked for readings,
after which they crossed her palm with silver.
Each sought to outdo the other in favors to the
gypsy, until one followed a donation of an earring with an entire necklace, which excessive-
ness would, she imagined—in the manner of
such ladies—make her superior to her sisters.

This ended matters. The ladies' readings were nothing like mine; the usual flattering and ambiguous predictions, having to do with lovers and husbands and the glorious future of their children.

But I believed her and have always approached the year 1815 as if it were a doorway through which I shall inevitably pass. While this has given my life its limit, it has also given me an ease and freedom, whatever the vicissitudes of my fate, for I knew that nothing could injure me before my time. The year 1815, she said, would be a year of marvels. I await my final removal with equanimity, my nephews and nieces not far distant, which is the reason I moved here. Having family around during the final years—no matter how venal they may be, though mine are not—gives us solid ground from which to ascend to the spheres where the spirit will finally circulate in that universal fluid where past and future are one, enclosed in the eternal now as it moves with the speed of thought from moment to moment, marking eternity as it replaces itself in great leaps and bounds, which is only another way of saying that time stands still. For there are no contradictions where the magnetic fluid, to which I have devoted my life, becomes the common substance in which we have our being.

But back to this earth, where the canary still stands on the rim of my drinking glass, hopping off when I raise it to my lips. Sometimes, curious as a lover, it hops onto the top of my head and, holding on tightly with its claws to my wig (and sometimes, when I am not wearing it, to the hazardous sphere of my vertex), peers down to watch the glass's tilted oval approach my lips. I am happy here. This is the last place I shall settle. I need a place from which to depart. Most of humankind has that desire, except for nomads and gypsies who carry their place around with them.

When my thoughts were in Paris with that gypsy, I was trying to remember when it was, in relation to other events. Was it before the lost dog? Or was it just after that damned Commission met? Or when the story about Marie Thérèse went around, so convincing in its falsehood that I half believed it myself?

As always when her image appears, my mind pauses and reflects on her, for apart from her affliction there was something in her nature that spoke to some aspect of mine, as if we shared a secret, transmitted through a vibration in the magnetic fluid. I still hear the sound of her piano, a little too ornate perhaps, even in memory, but how gifted, how gifted. She was doubly famous—as my patient and as a performer, though I hear she rarely performs now, devoting herself to teaching at some school which, I believe, she has founded in Vienna. I have no doubt that she is an excellent teacher, since she has great patience and much tenacity. Though I never again saw her after I left Vienna, rumor will not accept this. When I lived in the Place Vendôme, she performed in Paris at the Concert Spirituel, but I did not go. Rumor, of course, has it that I was present and was confounded as she was led to the piano, blind as blind could be. Indeed, rumor has certified this fiction as fact. Several have sworn they saw me at the theater. How convenient is this delusion! Every eye, according to this novelette, turned to me in my box as all Paris saw she could not walk unaided to the piano. I turned pale and immediately left without waiting for the performance. Of course she was blind, since the matter was in her organ's function, not in its structure, and that function was occluded by her circumstances, if we can call her parents "circumstances." Her parents may have been still alive then.

They are probably dead now, and, if retrospect can be forgiven a moment of indisposition, this subtraction has not greatly reduced the sum of the world's riches.

That moment of my nonpresence has become an accepted fact. I have met people who were at that concert and who speak to me discreetly of my disappointment, and when I protest I was not there, smile and change the subject. Yet over the years, the most peculiar thing has happened. I find myself beginning to concur with those witnesses who vouch for my presence. For my mind—and how biddable is the mind—has generously supplied vivid images of my presence. I see myself in the box, looking eagerly at the stage. I see Marie Thérèse enter, looking pale, a little older, led by a gentleman in black from throat to toe, with silver buckles and a peruke, his face powdered and pallid in the footlights.

She holds herself straighter than the anxious comma which once described her posture, a comma which, as in a sentence, bespoke her former hesitation. I hear the slight swish, as if the audience's body were clothed in a single garment, as every pair of eyes in the house turns towards me. I wait long enough to see her sit at the piano, fumble for the edge of the seat, and draw from the piano a few experimental notes, barely audible as she finds her key. She sits back, prefacing her performance with a long silence that doubly draws my attention to her person. But the audience's eyes remain on me, as if the theater were a vast lens converging all these parallel rays upon my person. I see myself confused between embarrassment, anger, and contempt for men's folly—blaming me for what in their crude estimates they could not know. I see myself, like truth itself, hounded and pursued. With dignity, I gather myself and rise, after returning, in one sweep of my eyes across the crowded house, that accusing collective gaze.

So vivid is this fiction that sometimes I have believed it true, as one does a dream that convinces for a few minutes, or even a day, so that one adjusts one's thoughts to it and rearranges one's past accordingly. Where was I, I ask myself, when my other self was serving the public need for my humiliation? I have no idea. My real self can offer no alibi. Taking a stroll in the Luxembourg? Working on my journal? Magnetizing some unfortunates? Receiving some of my visitors? At dinner? I have no idea. How many of our experiences, I wonder, are provided to us by an imagination which is ever eager to report on ourselves in situations from which we have been absent but which, in terms of poetic truth, certify themselves with conviction. So my history at that moment divides into two histories in which the real events are banal and forgotten and the fictional ones thoroughly convincing to the world at large, and even, in moments of inattention, to myself.

This event which I have described must have been *after* the gypsy marked my future with its terminus, for I seem to remember, without much conviction, the ladies whispering and gossiping about Marie Thérèse while looking expectantly at me as if I would respond—though this may be a fiction conveniently provided by my memory. Memory is about the great division of before and after, but some events cluster in the mind. I was trying to remember the year the gypsy made her prophecy, but at the same time, the dog, Marie Thérèse, and that wretched Commission, which, I suppose, was the deepest injury to my career, all come to mind at once. Though as I look back on the perspective of my life, some dates are as stable as rocks: 1778, the year I came to Paris, and 1784, the year of that Commission the King set up to please my enemies. Yet with age, even these begin to move,

occluding vistas and opening others that are
indistinct and often empty, but which desire
to be filled with memories true or false. At
times I experience the present more deeply
that ever before. Casual matters, like this canary, or when the wind whisks across the water
causing it to shiver as if the lake had suddenly
felt the cold—these are joys to me without
anything beyond their joy. I forget them the
next minute and then occupy myself trying to
remember the cause of this pleasant feeling. I
console myself that there is virtue in this exercise, because if I had truly forgotten, I would
not be trying to remember. My senses now
fold themselves around the moment, without
any responsibility to past or future, to possess
an experience that, like the moment itself,
does not last. My nose is too close to the window to see what is on the glass; I see far-off
things very clearly, incidents in which I observe, with some discomfort, my former self,
who seems quite an independent fellow. These
plays that memory enacts for me, sometimes
so clear in their details that I can almost smell
them, jostle for placement in the right se-
quence. Memory has its own space and time,
in which it marks, as in a familiar landscape,
its places, to which we return again and again

over a lifetime. Recently, as I say, they tend to step out of place, to play leapfrog and hide, so that the landscape is topsy-turvy, yet full of familiar things. I spend much time trying to replace them, taking my bearings from other events which, however, are often similarly afflicted.

I mentioned the dog. I remember to the minute, but not the day, when Antoine returned from his errands followed by that dog, a gray poodle, though some idiot kept insisting that it was an Airedale. But poodle it was, a gray poodle, and how can one mistake it, for they are all over the nobles' houses, while the court ladies favor the little papillon from Spain, which they sometimes carry in the bosom of their dress with the head sticking out, and sometimes the tongue sticking out of the head. The poodle would not go away. I went out to make friends with it, which is usually easy for me since animals are aware, particularly horses, birds, and dogs, that I know their secret. But he would have none of me, backing away, head lowered, tail between legs, as if ashamed. He showed no anger or fright, but wagged his tail weakly a few times. He would not let me touch him nor would he come inside when Antoine offered him food. The dog had his mind fixed on staying where he was, and nothing would entice him indoors, though he always followed Antoine on his errands. He stayed outside even in the snow, waiting for Antoine to appear. The mystery was resolved when Antoine was taking my letter to a friend on the rue d'Orleans. When he went into a shop to seek directions, the dog, as always, settled himself outside. Antoine was within when he heard the dog, whose name we never knew—we simply called him "dog," to which he learned to answer in a skeptical way, to judge by his ears—make a great commotion, leaping and barking and racing back and forth under a window where a man was leaning out and showing, but in the manner of our own species, a similar delight.

The dog, vigilant for over six weeks, had found its lost owner. With the dog leaping up on him, this man told Antoine the story: he had raised the dog in Moscow, brought him to Paris a year ago, and lost him on his arrival. But where, I asked Antoine on his return, had the dog been for all but the six weeks of the year he spent at our door? How did he survive? And why did he fasten on Antoine as his guide to his lost master? Why did he never enter the house but stay outside in all weathers? These questions gathered themselves together over one answer: the dog knew, through that instinct that connects animals to nature's wisdom, that Antoine would lead him to his master. Of all the people in Paris, of all the myriad crowds he had encountered, he had recognized that Antoine had his master in his future, and he would wait and wait for that encounter. So he became Antoine's shadow.

After all, my name for my discovery was "*animal* magnetism," and animals, being part of nature, are connected, as I say, by instinct to the magnetic movements within the invisible fluid. Visitors remark on this canary since it will not leave my side, accommodates me in whatever way it is capable, drops a lump of sugar into my coffee each morning, a marvel to others but not to me. Animals often surprise us with their wisdom; their senses, connected to instincts unimpeded by our skepticism, often possess knowledge that logic would refute. But then, it is in the nature of logic to refuse what is not compatible with itself, thereby excluding from its operation an order of knowledge to which it must always remain alien. Thus logic knows itself and nothing beyond itself, since it lives within its own borders. In my early years, in my attempts to

convince my colleagues, I tried to make my
discoveries compatible with their systems of
knowledge—which my cures repeatedly confounded. So some believed and others were
never relieved of their disbelief. That non-
sensical Commission devoted itself to formal
inquiry in circumstances where the ghost of
an original thought would shiver and vanish.
I now reject modes of inquiry that preempt
their own investigation by setting standards of
evidence that exclude the truth.

. . .

I am much disturbed. Last night, after writing
on some aspects of my theory with precision,
I went to bed with the satisfaction that follows
when one has done something well. I fell
asleep at once on the edge of that great magnetic ocean that awaits us when we relinquish
our waking minds. I was swept away on its
noiseless tide into those blessed realms where
one's spirit anticipates its transcendence. As
sometimes in my dreams, I heard music, often,
I must say, young Wolfgang's. But this music
I did not recognize, though its style was familiar. My curiosity brought me to a quiet
corridor at the end of which was a lighted room
from which the music issued. I seemed to glide

down the corridor, unconscious of my motion
and with no feeling of unease or dread. Passing
quietly through the door, I was bathed in a
blaze of light from a profusion of candelabras.
In one corner, with her back to me, a young
woman was at the piano, her hands flying out
to the extremes of the keyboard and back as
she played. The nape of her neck was accentuated by her bent head, and that intimate
part, to which its possessor must remain per-
manently blind, seemed sweetly vulnerable as
it ran its single-fluted column from head to
shoulders. As I placed my hands upon her
shoulders, I recognized the music. It was the
Lied auf die Blindheit of Marie Thérèse, the
song of her blindness which she had composed
and played for me soon after I began her treatment. At that time, I was greatly moved. In
my dream I remembered my original response, even my effort to find in the music
something that related to its title, for we sometimes search for its illustration in the music. I
remember listening for the sudden eclipse of
the light treble by a slow rumble from the dark
base. Of course you can find anything in any
music if you look for it. As these thoughts occupied me in the dream, my hands, to my
horror, slipped from her shoulders to her

bosom. The pianist raised her hands from the keyboard, fingers spread wide; she stretched her head directly back so that I saw it upside-down from above. Marie Thérèse's expression was one of utter terror, the eyes again showing nothing but the whites, as if she were trying to look at me through her own skull and substance. The shock was so intense that I woke up with my heart beating in a flutter of irregularities. I had to cough and sit at the side of the bed panting for some unknown length of time.

The middle of the night is not the time to examine one's dreams, for they only become more vivid and disturbing. But such was the dream's convincing power that I began to castigate myself for what I had done, which I now believed had occurred. I cast my thoughts back over thirty years to my house in Vienna, thinking of the many occasions when I had placed my hands innocently on her shoulders. When had I transgressed? What had possessed me to take advantage of a young woman whose illness I was trying to relieve, and whose trust in me was absolute? For the rest of the night my sleep was fevered and restless, haunted by the deepest sense of shame.

The morning brought a peculiar struggle,

and my usual view of the lake brought me no comfort. For in the light of day I refuted the charges made in my dream. This had never happened. But a suspicion remained. I remembered that such charges had been made against me and my assistants by the narrow-minded and hateful. Being pure in my conscience, they had never disturbed me, for they referred to the sickness of their owners rather than to me. Now I was accusing myself with the same charges! Matters of the flesh had never tormented me. What was the cause of this appalling dream? What disturbance in the magnetic fluid had attracted such images when I lay defenseless in sleep? Was there some planetary aberration, as sometimes occurs, that had forced me to tell a lie to my sleeping self? I massaged neck and head from below upward to bring the fluids to a balance that had been—I hope momentarily—lost. I gathered the fluid towards the eyes through massaging temples and forehead. Though it was my inner eye that was producing these images, the eye that lifts its secret lid when we sleep, I hoped to affect it by soothing my daylight eyes. But a doubt has been placed in my mind, which, no matter how I rehearse my past, I cannot cast out. For a moment, I thought that

I must find Marie Thérèse so that she could confirm my innocence. I even thought of the difficulties of finding her—she still may travel from Vienna to Amsterdam or Berlin or Prague on her tours. Common sense, however, dismissed this notion. I never touched her profanely.

Perhaps these images have visited me because I have ventured in recent years into questionable areas where my belief has led me. I have abandoned the logic of science, which can only reflect its own assumptions and confirm its own methods. I am convinced (though I am a scientist) that we can learn from oracles and sybils and mountebanks, who live in a twilight that extends beyond the present into past and future. I do not mock seers and fortune-tellers. But these researches have their darker side, and perhaps it is this that has opened my sleep to these abhorrent visitations. I have gone beyond science in these later years, and this invites some disturbance of the imagining faculty. I am completely firm, however, about my theory. What I have done, the cures I have performed—and perform to this day—are their own proof, the "logic" of which I leave to others to decipher. I speculate freely and annoy many. I am willing to change

my theory, should anyone convince me. But
the results that need explanation do not
change, and I have produced results that have
distressed the envious. What we see and understand depends on our capacity for reflection. The surface of the lake is sometimes
blurred and wrinkled and opaque, but always
has the possibility of reflection when it is calm
and still. Like every fluid, including the magnetic fluid, it contains its own future and past.
Depending on the agitation or smoothness of
our minds, matters are blurred or clear, for
we cannot maintain the same degree of clarity,
of acute perception, at all times.

When in a somnambulist state, do we not,
as in our dreams, know more than in our waking? The lost dog knew the future and, without
the darkness of human logic, could feel the
tides of the magnetic fluid circulating through
every artery. Yet you laugh when I say that
animals can know the future. But what is your
explanation of the gray poodle? In the magnetized state doors become avenues, the past
reflects the future, the future visits the past,
and the present holds both in potency, two
unreal continents between which we spend
our time as time spends us. On the edge of
the present, time, like a miraculous fluid, runs

through us. Sometimes, its flow bears us forward enough for the immediate future to become a past we remember. There is nothing mysterious about this. The present is, after all, merely an interruption in the fluid, which can be affected by magnetism, as the iron filings gather themselves around the positive (past?) and negative (future?) poles. The inner sense that controls the somnambulistic state responds to magnetism as the eye does to light. This sense, which is not the same as our outward senses, can divine the secrets of body and mind, and of the mind's body—or, if you wish, of the body's mind, though these are not the same. In the states that I have induced, there is a mind that responds, a living entity that is and is not the person who returns from the trance. Even as you read this, my thoughts enter and become yours, no matter how briefly. I can sense your inner being because the fluid, the magnetic fluid that surrounds us, extends far beyond my life and yours and encloses us both, though we may no longer exist. How can anyone trained in the logic of medicine deal with such truths? My theories are startling, but no more so than my results. Perhaps my theories are wrong, but the burden of proof is no longer on me but on those who succeed us both. Posterity will not be influenced by our personal passions; the natural likes and dislikes within any group of men, will, like their flesh, dissolve. Then justice can show its face. I have learned that criticism responds as much to our physiognomy as to our ideas.

Of such prejudices I have had my fill. Nowhere were my methods and results so rudely treated as by that wretched Commission, made up, as always, of the most distinguished of men. How eminent they were, how mature in judgment, how rich in worldly knowledge, how certain of their own capacities, how confident in their charge as they pondered, appointed by a court that seemed as eternal as the pyramids: a Queen I thought my friend, a King who was born to be a King's valet, free-thinking nobles playing with ideas of what is natural in man, unhappy with the court but part of it, as if to criticize it absolved them from its abuses, of which they were, by nature and birth, a part. Such dissent is a toy with which the privileged divert themselves with ideas of justice and the rights of man, as they came across the ocean from the first Revolution. Of course all those right-thinking nobles were the first to go, clutching Liberty and Jus-

tice all the way to the guillotine, protesting,
"You misunderstand me, I am on your side,"
until they became the Revolution's broken
toys. I became that Commission's toy, as they
exercised their wit, making little jokes which
outside the chamber of inquiry wouldn't have
made a servant laugh.

It is the belief of reasonable men that the
foibles of individuals are, when joined in discourse with those of their fellows, compressed
by a common sense into a page on which truth
can write its name. Each mind has its shadows,
but we believe that together men who seek
truth illuminate each other's darknesses. But
I believe—and I have reason to—that groups
of men can support each others' delusions
while confident that they are in the realm of
truth and justice. From the collective brow of
many a Commission issue conclusions that a
peasant would find wanting, but which, given
the authority of distinguished persons in collective cogitation, carry conviction to those of
us who offer them respect, until our own feelings eventually assert themselves with that insistent inner voice that cannot be suppressed.
If we are deaf to this inner voice, our harmony
is disturbed and our natures sadly confused. I
think of that Commission as a single body with

many heads, a kind of hydra which stared with all its eyes at my cures and froze them in their tracks. Of the head of that body, that old fool Benjamin Franklin, what am I to say? He never answered my letter, and unanswered letters dangle unhappily in my memory. He must have been the same age that I am now. He had a way of seeking opportunities in any discussion to advance his own wit no matter how serious the occasion, and he sought everyone's good opinion while slyly exercising his own prejudices, a trick he carried out with great innocence, as if the double meaning of what he inferred could not be ascribed to an American, no matter how sophisticated. In a word, people decided to like him. He was a great pet with the ladies; he chatted with them as if none were safe, though his age insured it.

None of those admirable men were qualified to judge my work. Bailly was a fine astronomer, but he lost his head in the Terror; so much for stargazing. As for Lavoisier, where is his severed head now? Collecting taxes? He should have stuck to chemistry. When he proposed that igneous fluid that binds all matter, did I scoff at this notion? But when I proposed the universal fluid, he disallowed it. As for Dr.

Guillotin, his name has dropped into history with a sinister thud, though the fool was a philanthropist who believed there should be a democracy in death for high and low alike, and that there should be no hierarchy in executions. Well, he barely missed being clipped by his own barber.

Commissions! Commissions! So many inquiries, judgments, investigations. My past is littered with them. So much intrigue, so many lies, so much blindness and malice, so much hatred for what may, even remotely, disturb the comfort of those who rule. A court cannot be transgressed from without by presumption, or from within by desertion. Mutual agreement confines its members. And this is true of societies of doctors, lawyers, and the like. Who threatens one of them, threatens all. My fate was always to be on the outside, seeking justice from those incapable of giving it. For whatever the acclaim of my patients—many and often distinguished, though they were—a border remained in place. The envy of those who hate me is composed, in part, of fear for their sacred professions, to maintain the integrity of which, in their estimate, stands above the good my discoveries would offer mankind. They keep mankind hostage to antique ideas of mind and body and disallow without a qualm the proofs I have offered, living proofs, which can be refuted only by an inner blindness so profound that it darkens the name of science. And then, to add insult to the injury, they reported: It is not your cures we disallow, it is your ideas about your cures; these are unacceptable! As if the evidence were fatally flawed by a false idea. I maintain my idea because I have not seen it displaced by another that convinces me. I am open to conviction. I do not close my eyes on my own system, though its results make it, to my mind, irrefutable. Remembering these fools and knaves so disturbs me that I must go to the window and ponder the lake with more equanimity than I ponder my past. If my inner state were now conveyed to these waters, they would become agitated with whirlpools of distemper, rippled with wavelets of acid. I must calm myself, which has been my command to myself for so many years.

When my mind is agitated in this fashion, it seeks, like an animal, every injustice with which the ignorance of men has afflicted me, and worries it to distraction. The result is a heavy and unpleasant distemper that can last for an entire day. At such moments I seek calming thoughts, memories of music and pleasure, of miracles wrought, and kindnesses offered and received. Sometimes I fill my glass harmonica with fresh fluids and play, though I miss the company of others then, and generally have little impulse to play as I did almost every day in Vienna. Wolfgang used to encourage me, for his bright and vivid face itself was enough to banish anyone's misery, a fact my good friend, his father, used to hold against him, as if he did not fully understand the seriousness of life. Wolfgang would make you try anything, and find pleasure in it, and those moments when he and Marie Thérèse played together are ones I cherish, for he made her play more directly, with fewer flourishes, as if she were the theme which he annotated with witty variations, sometimes running into such flights of invention and fancy that she would laugh so much she could not continue to play her more sober part.

When my memory trips on her, her face, beautiful in its smoothness and expression, with eyes downcast so that the spheres of her lids make her appear blind as a statue, sometimes suffices to discharge my dark mood. I try to think of her more often these days, since by remembering her as she was, I feel that I will prevent her visiting me in my dreams. I have rehearsed my memory, examined my conscience, and can find no occasion when my fatherly concern for her could be misconstrued. Yet these dreams have given me an Achilles heel, a doubt which, like an eager seed, is always ready to grow when my mind tempers its vigilance. My thoughts of her can rarely remain pure, for her dreadful family tend to accompany her and remain to find new ways to irritate me. One such occurred the other day, and detained her father's image. I could not remember his first name. It has always been available to me. But suddenly it was absent. His features, his arrogant nostrils, his variable eyes, were as clear as my own face in a mirror. Even his high-pitched voice was in my ear. But his name—his first name —was gone. This vacancy, this void, this unnatural eclipse of his Christian—or, rather, unchristian—name gave me no peace, since my mind attempted obsessively to fill in his first name in front of the signature "Paradies," which seemed to be visible to me simultaneous to his damned face. I had a certainty about the name, and could conduct its syllables like a piece of music without words. Two syllables: *Uh-uh* Paradies. Or *Uh-Oh-uh* Paradies? A kind of knot of syllables hovered in the vicinity, eager to untangle themselves and write his name. The feeling of his name was like a little pregnancy, but what was delivered to me was the feeling of an "A." This was how his name began. I knew it. But an Alexander? No. An Albert. That seemed closer. I tried each with the Paradies, but my mind said no. I attempted to relieve myself of this task by turning my back on it and thinking about something else, hoping the name would steal unnoticed into my mind. But it refused. Alexander and Albert did not go with the Paradies. Of that I was certain. Then I had it. It was Johann.

I felt a flush of satisfaction. Johann Paradies. The A was wrong. How could it have suggested itself? And been entertained as possible? Johann Paradies. But then, my mind, in studying the full name, found in it a discord, like a piece of music we remember but not exactly. Johann was right, but it was also wrong. My irritation at my unobliging mind became intense. I pictured the wretch as strongly as I could, with his wife, with his daughter. I reenacted scenes as in a play, but the main actor's first name remained uninscribed on my program. He himself was enjoying my frustration, or so I fancied. Paradies, Johann, Johann. But the J was right. And then, like a firework arching into the air, his name burst into my mind with exhilaration and relief: Josef! Josef! Josef Paradies! It confirmed itself for accuracy at once. And my memory, with which I had been unfriendly, commended itself to me. I was released for a moment from my own stupidity.

But the stupidity of others never ceases to exasperate my nature, even now, when I know my justification lies far beyond my death. I have never accepted the fact that the Commission, the findings of which changed my life, did their work without me, never talked to me, never examined my patients, never solicited a demonstration from me, and yet found my method wanting. It was not my clinic they investigated, but d'Eslon's. Why go to my pupil when the master is at hand? I was visiting in Switzerland for much of that time, but I would have come back posthaste if d'Eslon had even whispered my name. The entire matter is still a mystery to me. When I met with the Queen, I thought I had made my case successfully. We shared a regard for her sainted mother, the Empress Maria Theresa of Austria, whose recent passing distressed us both. The Empress's name brought back thoughts of my exit from Vienna and of the Paradies family. I remember that Paradies told me several times of the Empress's concern for her Frenchified daughter, whose arrogance (he said) further compressed a nature already thin as a wafer. When d'Eslon and I went to see her about a formal examination and recognition of my method, Marie Antoinette seemed discomforted by my passion for my ideas. She hid behind her royal distance, playing with the papillon in her lap, favoring d'Eslon with her glances when she was not looking out at the gardens where her ladies were moving in that idle way of theirs, like swans.

She offered me everything—a pension, a practice, a building—if I would take on pupils who would be assigned to me and teach them my method. And this, of course, as I explained to her in a letter, I had, in justice to myself, to refuse. They would spy on my ideas and inmost thoughts, take my discoveries and give them, misshapen, to the world without my signature. I alone should select and train my own followers, as Bergasse was always saying. I did not seek pensions and institutes. I wanted only one thing: the royal imprimatur on my method, and sufficient funds to pursue it. I told her as much in that letter which d'Eslon said treated her royal person with a lack of respect unbecoming a commoner. But those in high places need to be reminded from time to time of their mortal status, having two eyes and ears and a face like the rest of us, and possessing no privileged knowledge at birth, since kings and queens are born as innocent as the rest of us. Nor did she respond to d'Eslon's request for the appointment of a Commission that would justify my discoveries, although he had already spoken of it to the King's physician—de Lassonne, I think his name was. D'Eslon was everywhere, making representations in his French manner, and doing it without me, to my chagrin. When I pointed this out, he said again and again—I am setting the stage on which you, the Master, will play your part.

But matters changed after my letter to Marie Antoinette, and my instincts have never lied to me. D'Eslon was more distant after that letter. He withdrew from me his confidence, not by word or gesture or disregard for my opinions. If you observe closely, these things can be noticed in significant trifles. He no longer faced me directly when he spoke, but pointed a shoulder at me, with head slightly turned, not always meeting my eye. He was meticulously polite as always, but a shade too much so. For a time we dismiss such perceptions, for we cannot bear to think ill either of our friends or of our own judgment. How strange that d'Eslon, and not myself, became the arbiter of *my* fate when he presented *his* cases, and not mine, to these wretched Commissions, for finally there were two of them, one was not enough, as I remember. I see d'Eslon now, forty years later, in a prevailing image that immediately comes to mind when my inner voice spells out his name. I see not the many moods of that face, but a single expression which has the same relation to the features as mind to body. That expression describes the final judgment we make on friends and enemies alike, if we pause to read it. D'Eslon's expression, as I pursue it now, is, above all, neutral. In memory's mirror, he does not look at me but fixes his gaze to his right as if he thought there might be something of interest there that turned out not to be; his brows are slightly knit, as if examining a problem more puzzling than difficult. His head is tilted back slightly, turned to bring out the long neck muscle. He looks like a man the ladies would desire but who has no great time for them. In a word, his apparition is slightly cold, and very French. But then, my judgments are made from a birthright I cannot alter, my own ardent nature.

D'Eslon accomplished what I could not: the appointment of the Commissions, and this, though it was in my interests at the time, did not make my feelings for him warmer. He did not allow me to present the proofs to the Commissions; I suspect he felt I would hurt my own cause, for my impatience urges me ahead of those I would convince. What was the name of that second Commission? The first was the Academy of Sciences. How we forget matters essential to us at the time . . . It was, my memory now hastens to oblige me, the doctors, my friends the doctors, the Royal Society of Medicine. Among them but one noble scientist whose name I honor—de Jussieu. His classification of plants is one of the wonders of taxonomy, bringing the mind's order into nature's profusion. De Jussieu was a man of marvellous insight, skill, and moral energy. Alone among those fools he perceived what they could not: he saw the results and could not explain them away in a manner satisfactory to himself. He observed the mystery of the crisis and the trance, and he held to a position rare among those who claim to be fair and just examiners: suspend judgment, accumulate results from several sources, weigh the evidence, and do not issue opinions from predispositions that exclude the possibility of perceiving truth.

Poor de Jussieu! Alone among those beasts in that Commission's kennel. He could have been stronger than he was, but surrounded by the prejudices of others, how could he? The case was closed before it was opened. The favor of the Queen was lost, the second Queen in that family to treat me harshly, though I do not bear the mother a grudge. The King, laughing at those satires and burlesques on the stage deriding my methods. The medical profession, threatened by my cures. And what allies did I have, apart from d'Eslon, Bergasse, and a few others? Noble ladies and the poor, which it is not possible to combine into a force. But there, the tense has changed as I relive it: which it *was* not possible to combine.

What stories came back to me, from several sources, about that Commission! It was beneath my pride to await d'Eslon's reports with cap in hand at his front door. What a comedy this tragedy became! They all took themselves, full of judicious gravamen, out to the old fool at Passy, Franklin. D'Eslon magnetized him and the rest of the Commission—a mass magnetism, which I would not have done. What happened should have been on the stage. It was more a farce than that burlesque, *Modern Doctors*, which made that mad supporter of mine, d'Éprémesnil, so crazed he went to the Comte d'Artois to force him to take it off the boards. No, this solemn farce was more entertaining. I cannot imagine circumstances less conducive to doing my discoveries justice. The mind and its buoyancy in the eternal fluid, the invisible magnetized sea, the universal substance that we share with all life and which permeates all matter—how could that be manifested among a group of rationalists who did not relish my person? It would be easier to catch a butterfly in an empty glove.

What a group of intelligent oafs! X was magnetized but failed to respond. Y was not magnetized but responded. D'Eslon was asked to magnetize a blindfolded woman and failed. Some other fellow pretended to magnetize her and she trembled and went into spasms. Several of them watched d'Eslon lay his hands on old Bailly, and asked him if he felt the fluid enter him, which they thought it might when he gave a shiver, but he, irritated, explained that it was not magnetism but a draft from the window; d'Eslon tried again and nothing happened. What a crowd of circus animals, staggering around amidst yokels and servants brought in as subjects, examining themselves and each other! If magnetism had a face, it would have shown exasperation and amusement. For the fluid was rudely summoned, mocked, eclipsed by this fellow's opacity and that fellow's skepticism.

The fluid, as I see it with my mind's eye, is a smooth, transparent substance, uniform in density, which disturbs nothing as it hands its effect from atom to atom, as one sees a twig bob in the circles of a pond when one has thrown a stone. The twig does not move from its place, but shudders as the wave lifts it and passes on. I see the substance in terms of my senses, though no sense can discern it—we know it only through its effects. I often see it as a luminous sheath of weightless extension which binds the stars and our souls in one glowing substance, a substance which has within it a perfect stillness, yet is itself motion in potency, a motion that can be urged to concentrate in our bodies by the hands of the magnetic physician. It is subtle and indifferent, the benign arbiter of our existence as we wax and wane in the cycles of earth and

planets, which inscribe their elipses and tri-
angles, their elastic and glorious geometries,
in the luminous fluid that encompasses all matter and spirit. And these fools said, as they
said to Newton and Huygens, *I cannot see it.*

If this invisible agent, said they, causes
changes in our bodies, then where is it? If it
exists, our senses or our instruments could ap-
ply themselves to it. So they brought an elec-
trometer to the baquette. If we cannot record
it with instruments or with our own faculties,
they said, then its existence requires an act of
faith, and as scientists, faith belongs to a previous age to which your animal magnetism
would return us. I have held to my fluid as
Newton held to his subtle matter. I have rejected, as d'Eslon properly did, explanations
which attribute my cures to the patient's
imagination, febrile fancies, hysteria, self-
intoxication, credulousness, and to those poor
half-sisters of science, occultism, fakery, and
magic. They wish to disallow the scientific nature of my invention, reducing it to magic and
quackery. They cannot see that the magnetic
fluid is the medium of all healing; it is the
denominator of all living matter. My work has
carried forward a vision of a world in which all
living things are in harmony, in which good is

the absence of evil as health is the absence of sickness. That power is there for us to use or misuse. I shudder at the disharmonies that now throw Europe into discord, as that Corsican ogre conquers the world, substituting his own terrible harmony, as if the planets had been darkened by his black sun. To such perversions is the spirit of man, when attracted by the negative poles of greed and power, drawn.

How could I abandon my notion of a world in harmony to mountebanks and fakes? I offered not just cures and remedies, but a vision of our better nature. My work was adapted by the Revolution, but that vision of mankind free and equal became a perversion of freedom and equality, breeding forth this monster. I wish to be left in peace to add to the community of harmonious spirits as I have for over forty years. That spiritual community consoles me now: old and young, rich and poor, men and women, children, hopeless cases, courtiers, farmers, fellow doctors, scientists. My supporters never fully understood the larger vision, but contented themselves by relaying my magnetic energies to their cures, so that my history branches like a tree with students and followers, each in turn magnetizing and curing. That community of cures I perceive as one hears music, spirits in harmony with the orbs and spheres as they circulate through the eternal fluid. What part of mankind does this community compose? A fraction indeed. But is it not a beginning to the reformation of mankind that would eliminate distempers, meanness, hatred, wars? How could I allow them to reduce my science to personal magic? To make of me the mountebank they sorely wished me to be?

My cures, they said, were due to the patient's imagination exercising itself beneficially. They even concluded that if an illusion heals, do not remove the illusion, for that will remove the cure. On that insulting basis they would accept my results. They did not even allow me to present my own cases. How bitter that is to this day! D'Eslon, my disciple, presents my theory while I stand helpless outside! If I would admit that my results, as explained by d'Eslon, were due to the imagination, they would accept them. But not my theory. They would accept anything but the truth that would vindicate my method and place it in the medical pharmacopeia. What an alternative they placed before me! Abandon my theory and call off the attacks of those medical colleagues who

now persecute me. Or persist and continue to
suffer their ignorance and contempt. I could
be a successful magician or a despised col-
league. They asked me to drink the poison of
their approval. How seductive to a weaker
spirit. But I have not failed my vision, and I
maintain it, stronger than ever, to this day. As
I wrote to Franklin—he never replied—I retain my integrity as strong men retain theirs
under authority. My last word to him is written
on my mind so clearly that I see my hand—
my hand at twenty years remove—form the
letters: *I will be vindicated by posterity.*

And so today history, equally tardy and premature, sends me intimations of my vindication in the person of that young German,
Wolfart, from the Academy of Science in Berlin, to show respect for me and to honor my
method. When you place a truth in the world,
it can never be fully suppressed.

Do you think I inflate my methods, my results, my hopes and certainties? I do not have
such general thoughts when I am with a patient. The grand vision may hover in the background, but it is not in one's immediate mind.
The treatment you devise, though it stems
from the theory and gains certainty from it,
fully occupies the foreground of one's atten-

tion. In the most difficult cases, my inner certainty has been the great source of confidence and calm, even with what the ignorant judge as failures. For some cases do not answer to my method when the fluid is resistant and I am unable to attract and mold it to the affected part or faculty. Sometimes the organ is so injured, it is beyond repair. Sometimes the influence of others on the patient so confuses them that the fluid is agitated and cures reverse themselves.

Some cases of this nature remain in my mind from my early days. I think particularly, of course, of the young Marie Thérèse. I see her face now—the involuntary cause of my departure from Vienna, though no blame can attach to her for that. How that case has followed me! And how it follows me to this day—or night— in those dreams that have so disturbed the equilibrium of my fluids. Sometimes I have a premonition that I shall dream of her, or rather that the outrageous fiction that has invaded my sleep will use me to dream itself. I try to forestall this dream by thinking of her in the most positive way, innocent and radiant in her happier moments. I massage my neck and temples to move the fluid to my closed eyes, so that when my inner eye opens in a dream it does not observe the falsities and lies it has presented to me before. Sometimes this effort is successful and I pass the night in blissful repose.

But not yesterday. I went to bed after ministering to myself, but a feeling of oppression remained. In my sleep I found myself again in the dark corridor leading to the blazing rectangle of the lighted room. I heard her voice, accompanying herself on the piano, singing her *Lied auf die Blindheit*. Against my will I found myself propelled along the corridor towards the music. No matter how much I resisted, I was forced to approach the doorway. As I was about to reach it, the music stopped. In silence I was forced through the door into the light. I thought to oppose my dream, and the force with which it controlled me, by closing my eyes. A blessed darkness, or rather a red misty twilight, replaced the light. But then, inexorably, as if my lids weighed a ton but were being raised by a greater force, my eyes were opened. She stood before me, entirely naked, her body, still half childish with young breasts and scanty sex, sheathed in light, so that I was almost blinded after the darkness of the corridor. Her eyes, no longer blind, but huge and without expression locked

onto my own. She had a slight smile in which
I could find no clear expression. She advanced
towards me without seeming to move, and I
found that the door behind me had vanished
and been replaced by a wall. In a great convulsion of effort, I reminded myself of my fatherly role and raised my arms in an open
gesture. Again I was propelled forward.
Reaching her, I closed my eyes and embraced
her reassuringly. Her body was fragile as a
sparrow's, and I had a feeling of triumph, as
if I had laid this dream and its wretched im-
plications to rest. But in the darkness, her
body filled out, her arms around me became
knowing and suggestive. Their caresses ap-
pealed to something dark in my being. In an
animal darkness, a violent passion seized me
of an order unknown to me in my prime. The
shock of this broke me out of the dream into
a waking state, where I remained for a time,
paralyzed. I found myself panting and exhausted with effort and anguish. After such
dreams I usually examine my conscience and
massage the fluids again to my brain. But this
time a different idea presented itself. I saw
myself, eighty years old, sitting in darkness at
the side of my bed, recovering and lusting after
a young girl of eighteen who was now a woman

of forty-five or -six, probably unremarkable in her looks, teaching composition and piano in a city three hundred miles away and at this moment probably asleep herself. The realization of this was so acute that I did not notice a strange contraction in my throat, followed by rhythmic spasms that shook my thorax. When I raised my hands to my face I found it wet. I was crying, and the desolation of this reinforced my misery, until my curiosity, always at hand for the scientist, observed this phenomenon, which must not have occurred for close to seventy years, and in the observance, stilled it.

I lay in bed, half in half out of this dream, until the new servant (why do I keep forgetting her name?) brought my morning drink of hot water. Recollection added to Marie Thérèse's face those of her dreadful mother, her wretched father. My mind proceeded to offer me further shocks. Had vile thoughts of his daughter and myself entered his mind? He was jealous and over-fond of her, that was clear. Had some monstrous thoughts in his own mind been ascribed to me? I have seen this before. People sometimes attribute their own unacceptable desires to others, whom they then attack. It is a way of getting rid of such embarrassments. But all this was so long ago. Yet memory has made it vivid. Why should it return under the disguise of truth when I know it to be false?

Memories of my friends from those distant days began to reassure me, as did the plate and glass before me. Their very substance anchored me to the present. I saw in my mind's eye the calm, restraining presence of Comte de Pellegrini, for whom I had a particular affection. Where he is now, God knows. It is strange how the past returns. If we do not revisit it, it tends to evaporate like water under the sun. Some pools of reflection remain. There memory lurks in images which, with further recollection, recall their origin, though we do not know (witness my frightful dreams) how "true" they may be, or how they fit themselves to our needs and expectations. What we remember is constantly changing as we are borne forward in the long perspectives of time. Both memory and ourselves are in motion as we regulate our past to give some meaning to the accidents of life that have befallen us.

But why should memory now lie to me? If this lie convinced me, then all my past was vulnerable. Who knows what part of my life this internal demon would next attack.

Through the window, the lake was obscured
with morning mist. For all I could tell, monsters might be rearing up from its depths,
men-of-war might be engaged in a silent battle, whirlpools might be sucking down their
ships. Might be, might be. Anything might be.
All my life, evidence has been confounded by
the doubt of others. Now that doubt has entered the chambers of my own mind and heart.
That is why I write and reform my theories in
my journal. For once the words are there, external to myself, they can be judged by my
colleagues and by the future, for the future
holds my vindication. Suddenly I recalled that
I had written an account of the sad end of the
case of Marie Thérèse. There, written in the
past, was my vindication. That text would
convince the most important witness—myself
—of my innocence. I could put down that insurrection within my memory, and regain the
peace appropriate to my age and condition.
My burst of enthusiasm was overtaken by another frustration. Where was it? I had—as I
had many other documents in my travels—
mislaid it. But a miracle, if you would account
it that, helped me find it. A magic sprite, that
canary which absurdly attends me (I am sure
it will not long survive me) perched, while

these thoughts were exercising me, on the knob of the lowest drawer of my bureau, and began to sing as if it were morning. The perch was an awkward one, and I noticed it, half-abstracted, since my eyes were on my memory-theater. It was only the oddness of the perch, and the singing, which had at first irritated me, that made me curious. I bid the bird come to me, but it would not. I arose, went across the room, and, bending down, held out my finger beside the knob, which, however, the canary refused to leave. I gathered the bird in with my other hand and placed it on my head—a favorite place—where it kept singing, too close to my ear. What made me open the drawer, I do not know. Before a drawer, I suppose, one's instinct is to open it. It was, to my memory, a dead drawer, paralyzed with storage, as befitted one so inaccessible by reason of the bending that now sent the blood unpleasantly to my head.

As I turned over the papers inside that musty hollow, a little graveyard of the past, I began to spread some of them on the floor with the vague idea of getting my effects in better order. From the back of the drawer, where one might expect something elusive and long-forgotten to be, I extracted a folded manuscript

in the handwriting of my Vienna days. It remained foreign to me as I read the first few
lines, but a phrase, and then a name, suddenly
acquainted me with the matter. The entire
document became familiar. I held in my hand
the testimony of a prime witness in the Paradies case: myself. (I did not neglect to reward
the bird with its favorite grain, which it consumed, looking at me with abrupt jerks of its
head from side to side, presenting one eye and
then the other, as it raised its beak from the
feeder. Its second sight represented to me
again the mysterious ways in which the magnetic fluid penetrates both animal and human
thoughts, so that when its waves and motions
are in consonance, transference between man,
beast, and bird is possible.)

I began to read the manuscript with curiosity and trepidation. It was strange to me, its
details long-forgotten. I found that I had neglected to describe my first meeting with
Marie Thérèse, or to give an account of my
first treatments. These now have been sucked
into oblivion, the forgetting which, far from
passive, is a consuming force that, gathering
strength, eventually overtakes us all. I read
with urgency as the evidence of this earlier
less, myself, began to displace and reform

my memories. So in reading I had a sense of double displacement from both my present and my past, as if a third party were reading and listening to my earlier self speaking in the present tense of a present long perished. The reading of the manuscript was thus not a simple matter, since I was aware of several processes taking place as I read, with some phrases touching off bursts of memory that returned me to the darkened room in Vienna. I disciplined myself to read steadily, avoiding my impulse to skip and search for evidence that would exonerate me. My first mention of her was mild enough:

After returning to Vienna in 1776, I refused to undertake any further work until the end of that year. I would not have changed my mind if my friends had not been unanimous in opposing my decision. Their urging aroused in me a desire to see the truth prevail. This I felt I could accomplish through some striking cure. I undertook the treatment of Mlle. Paradies, aged eighteen, whose parents were well known; she herself was known to Her Majesty, the Queen-Empress, through whose bounty she received a pension, being quite blind since the age of three. She had a perfect amaurosis, with convulsions in the eyes. She was also *a prey to melancholia, accompanied by stop-pages in her spleen and liver, which often brought on attacks of delirium and rage. She was convinced she was out of her mind.*

She reappeared again a few pages later . . .

The father and mother of Mlle. Paradies, who witnessed the progress she was making (why did I not describe her cure?) *in the recovery of her eyesight, hastened to make this occur-rence widely known. Crowds flocked to my house* (a few dozen at most, and these not all at once; my enthusiasm then may have led me to multiply) *to see the cure for themselves. Each one, after putting the patient to some kind of test, withdrew greatly astonished, with the most flattering remarks to myself.* True, indeed. I remember many compliments to my method.

The two Presidents of the Faculty (of Med-icine, of course) *with a deputation of their col-leagues came to see me at the repeated insistence of M. Paradies. After examining the young lady, they added their tributes to that of the public. Dr. Stoerk* (ah, false friend!) *knew this young person particularly well, having treated her for ten years without the slightest success. He expressed to me his satisfaction at so remarkable a cure and his regret at having deferred his acknowledgment of my discovery. A number of physicians followed his example and paid the same tribute to truth.*

After such confirmation, M. Paradies was kind enough to express his gratitude in a written report, which went all over Europe. He also published details of his daughter's recovery in the newspapers. I have them somewhere also. *Among the physicians who came to satisfy their curiosity was Dr. Barth* (infamous fellow!), *cataract specialist and professor of the anatomy and diseases of the eye. On two occasions he had admitted to me that Mlle. Paradies was able to use her eyes. Nevertheless his envious nature prompted him to state publicly that he had satisfied himself that the young lady could not see. He insisted that she did not know the names of objects shown to her. Everyone told him he was confusing the inability of those blind from birth to know what they were looking at with the knowledge remembered by blind persons operated on for*

*cataract, whose memories of sight are intact.
How, he was asked, can a man of your distinction be guilty of so obvious an error? His
impudence, however, found an answer to
everything. In vain he was told again and
again that a thousand witnesses had testified
to the cure; he alone persisted in holding the
opposite view, in which he was joined by
Ingenhousz.*

I still wonder at the nature of their hatred
for me. Whence its source? Does all the
world's envy issue from the same venomous
well? Though its expression may be different,
its physiognomy is always familiar. If I have a
fault that has injured me, it is the inability to
understand hatred, envy, malice—though
God knows I have had enough in my life to
make me an expert. There is a flaw in our
unmagnetized nature that seems, like a negative pole, to draw us to darkness, a flaw that
ignores differences in a man's estate, whether
rich or poor, favored or unfavored, Old World
or New—which latter gave us the first great
convulsion in our social order. I witnessed the
second with my own eyes, though sometimes
I wish I had myself been blind at that time,
for its images persist with a vividness that chas-

tises my thoughts, and in twilight moments often force me to rehearse that Terror with my private version of it.

These two individuals (Barth and Ingenhousz), *at first regarded as fanatics by sensible folk, wove a plot to withdraw Mlle. Paradies from my care. Her eyes were still in an imperfect state, making it impossible to present her to Her Majesty, as had been planned. This demonstration would have certified the truth of my method once and for all. The cancellation gave credibility to their charges. They worked on Paradies, who began to fear for his daughter's person, and to worry that advantages offered by a solicitous Majesty might cease.* Obviously it is the girl's pension I refer to here. *As a result of all this scheming, he asked that his daughter be returned to him at once.* I remember the fool standing before me, half embarrassed and half arrogant, referring —he no doubt thought discreetly—to his court connections, finally resolving his uncertainties in a kind of condescension, as if I were his servant.

Poor Marie Thérèse, supported by her mother (both were present at this foolishness), *was unwilling to depart from my care, ex-*

pressing a fear that the cure might be imperfect. The father insisted, and this dispute
brought on her fits again, leading to a relapse
in her general health. Fortunately this conflict
did not affect her eyes, and her use of them
continued to improve. When her general
health had been restored, the father—provoked by the conspirators—returned again.
He passionately demanded his daughter's return, and compelled his wife to do likewise.

The girl resisted (no wonder she had flourished out of the hands of these monsters!),
citing the same reasons as before. They departed. The following week the mother returned, apologizing for the lengths to which
her husband had gone. But she had, she con-
fessed, a change of heart. Hitherto she had
resisted her husband as best she could. But
now she informed me that on the 29th of April
(the year was 1777—I remember three sevens,
and seven had always been a number that comforted me) she herself intended to remove her
daughter from my care. I replied that she was
free to do so, but if the girl relapsed, she could
not count on my help.

This was overheard by Marie Thérèse, who
was so overcome that she fell into a fit. She

was assisted by Comte de Pellegrini, one of my patients (I see his face). *Her mother, hearing the girl's cries, left me abruptly and in a fury seized her daughter, and, shouting "Wretched girl, you too are hand-in-glove with the people of this house!" flung her head-first against the wall. Immediately, all the troubles of that unfortunate girl recommenced. Only the whites of her eyes were visible, her body convulsed, and spittle flew from her mouth as she chewed and locked her jaw in spasms. I hastened to her assistance, but the mother, livid with rage and screaming insults, hurled herself upon me. She was removed from my person by members of my household, and I went directly to the girl's assistance. While so engaged, I heard angry shouts. The door of the room was half-opened and shut several times with some violence. It was M. Paradies, who had invaded my house, sword in hand. The madman was at last disarmed by my servants. As he left, still struggling, he breathed imprecations on myself and on my household. When I looked back into the room, the wretched wife, overcome by her emotions, was on the floor beside her daughter.*

From this distance, I can summon a particle of sympathy for the villain. Hearing his wife's cries, thinking his precious daughter a prisoner, what must he have thought? Coincidence, frequently so mischievous, had brought him to my door at the exact moment of his wife's distress. Yet he knew me well enough to know that in my hands no harm would come to wife or daughter. Though he was an obsequious and expert courtier, he suppressed an urgent, choleric nature. Impulse ruled him in intimate matters, and he must have felt that the privacy of his family had been cruelly violated. Did he see his wife swooned in the inner room as he departed? Did I err in so rudely separating him from her? I remember my anger that my work on the girl had all come to nothing as she returned to her darkness and distress. Did my anger lead me to win the moment at the cost of my future in Vienna? Did I underestimate Paradies's court connections? I certainly underestimated the power of gossip and its grotesque transformations, which represented the scene in ways that did credit to none of the parties involved, including myself. Forty years later I can contemplate these questions with some equanimity. But not then.

*I gave Mme. Paradies the necessary atten-
tion, and she left some hours later without her
daughter. The unhappy girl could not be
moved. She was suffering attacks of vomiting,
fits, and rages, which the slightest noise, especially the sound of bells, accentuated.*
(Bells? Of course! We were in the shadow of
St. Stephen's.) *Worst of all, she had relapsed
into blindness through the violence of her
mother's assault, and I had fears for the state
of her brain.*

Such (my report continues) *were the sinister
effects of that painful scene. I could easily have
taken the matter to court on the evidence of
Comte de Pellegrini and the eight other persons present. But as my sole concern was to
save Mlle. Paradies, if that were possible, I
refrained from seeking legal redress. My
friends disagreed, pointing out the parents'
ingratitude and the wasted expenditure of my
labors. I adhered to my decision and would
have been content to overcome the enemies of
truth and of my peace of mind by good deeds.
But next day I heard that M. Paradies, en-
deavoring to cover up his excesses, was spreading the most wicked insinuations regarding
myself, with a view to removing his daughter*

and ascribing her condition to the dangerous nature of my methods. Shortly thereafter, I personally received from Dr. Ost, Court Physician, a written order from Dr. Stoerk, in his capacity as head physician, dated "Schönbrunn, 2nd May 1777," which called upon me "to put an end to this imposture" (Stoerk's very expression!) "and restore Mlle. Paradies to her family," if I thought this could be done without risk.

Who would have believed that Stoerk, being fully informed by Dr. Ost of what had taken place in my house, and having paid two visits to verify the patient's progress and the success of my methods, would take it upon himself to use such offensive and contemptuous language with me?

I notice now, more clearly than I did then, that Stoerk placed a condition at my disposal: ". . . if I could send her back to her family without risk." Had I the good sense then that I have now, this injurious affair might have been negotiated through Stoerk. I could have gone to see him, citing our old friendship. But I was far too exercised at the tone of the letter. Its chilly official distance shocked me, and I did not stop to contemplate the forces that may

have been—I'm sure were—brought to bear
on him, leaving him little latitude but to write
as he did. At least he might have called on
me, or sent a private message to take the sting
out of the official one. As I look back, I see
that I responded not just to the text and tone
of the letter—though these were shocking to
me—but to the circumstances surrounding it.
The letter dropped into a net so highly sensitive that it vibrated with matters not strictly
contained within it. With such letters, I now
know, we respond not only to the injuries in-
flicted by the words, but to the way our minds
magnify and connect these words to matters
often quite remote from their substance. Into
the silence of what is *not* said but (we think)
implied, we even read—in our rush to inflict
upon ourselves further damage—unintended
rebukes and criticisms, thereby forfeiting the
possibility of applying to an unpleasant letter
a cool and reasonable eye. But even as I read
this letter again, and listening to my own coun-
sel, my gorge rises. This situation was already
befouled by too many dangerous factors, of
which the most lethal was the wretched Paradies influence at court. Who has the ear of
the Empress has us in his power. Had I the

ear of Her Majesty, I might have prevailed in my treatment, since she was a woman of true majesty and honor, much different from her French daughter, whose person and position were so violently removed from this world. My journal goes on:

I had reason to expect better from Stoerk. Being well placed to recognize the truth, he should have been its defender. I would even go so far as to say that as the repository of Her Majesty's confidence, one of his first duties under these circumstances should have been to protect a member of the Faculty whom he knew to be blameless, and to whom he had time and again given assurances of his affection and esteem. I answered this irresponsible order thus: My patient could not be moved without the risk of death.

With this I thought the matter immediately settled. But I underestimated the perfidy of my enemies. The poor girl had become a pawn in a game involving the court, the medical profession, my household, my friends and enemies, and their friends and enemies. The girl's struggles against her affliction, like those of a fly in a web, vibrated through the streets and thoroughfares of the city. The affair became entertainment for people who enjoy misfortunes that divert them from their own. They take pleasure in others' suffering, even more in their humiliation, and, once the balance tilts against one of two parties, add their weight to the prospective victor, the further to crush one who now seems defenseless. This phenomenon I would liken to animals who in the wild turn against one of their kind who has suffered injury, but the comparison dishonors animals, whose faithfulness far surpasses that of our own. I speak of balance. But it is, of course, the magnetic fluids that are imbalanced by such events when people together behave in a way that singly, one by one, they would not. For the fluid can be greatly influenced by the collective mind and seems to move more easily to the negative than to the positive pole. Indeed, in such situations those who do not join in the common prejudice are themselves endangered, for in withholding their concurrence, they are perceived by their fellows as assuming a superior pose, and must suffer the consequences of this offence.

In all of this suspicion, curiosity, and hatred, my first concern was for my patient. Her state was, as I had conveyed through Ost,

critical. This was known to everybody. Colleagues heard the matter directly from Ost,
and, if they didn't believe it, through their
servants. Marie Thérèse's fragile condition
was no doubt conveyed to her father from several sources, making it difficult for him to press
for her removal. Also, if he insisted in separating his daughter from her treatment, he
could be seen as contributing to her plight.
When matters touched his reputation at court,
his judgment was capable of careful discrim-
inations. He had to balance his reputation for
diligent subservience at court with the vicious
threats and abuse he had circulated. I was not
surprised when two reputable persons appeared at my door conveying a request from
Paradies that I continue to treat his daughter.

What was I to believe at this point? Had the
story of his entry to my house with drawn
sword injured his standing? Was he mollifying
me while continuing his campaign of lies and
deception? For this man was capable of so
many deceptions that I wondered how he could
keep one from rising up to contradict another.
He would shape a lie to suit any occasion, so
how could anyone pay attention to him? But
even as I asked the question, I knew the an-

swer. He had the Empress's favor. How could she trust him? Such wretches as Paradies flatter their patron, who, hearing what conforms to their desire, bestow their trust. Paradies also had the courtier's gift of conveying a matter distasteful to the Empress in such a way that she seemed to happen on the thought herself, seeking only confirmation from him, which he then reluctantly supplied. He had the courtier's nimbleness in full measure. He could sometimes so confuse matters with hints and inventions that everyone, friend or foe, having lost any sense of what the truth might be, in searching for it stirred up such a chaos that Paradies would quietly suggest a course which seemed like a reasonable solution to confused colleagues. He would then retire while some dupe took up that suggestion, believing it to be his own—even at times seeking out its originator to persuade him! In dealing with such people you must set your course clearly, so that your actions certify their worth by their consistency, no matter what provocations you may suffer.

I sent back word, in writing, to Paradies that I would continue to treat his daughter on condition that neither he nor his wife ever again appeared at my house. There was no written response to this; word was sent back to me that he desired nothing more than to have his daughter's health restored. I recommenced my treatment, and the results exceeded my hopes. After nine days, her fits subsided and her physical embarrassments ceased. But her blindness remained. After fifteen days of retracing the steps previously taken with such difficulty, her sight was returned to its condition prior to the incident. After a further two weeks, her general health was significantly improved. At that point, I allowed the public to confirm my second cure on her person. All visitors were convinced of her recovery, and several gave me, in writing, fresh evidence of satisfaction. Through Dr. Ost, Paradies followed the progress of our treatment, and being assured of the good health now enjoyed by his daughter, wrote a letter to my wife in which he thanked her for her motherly care. This epistle was followed shortly by another to me in which he apologized for the past. His letter concluded with a request, courteously stated, to return his daughter so that she might benefit from the air in their country home. He said he would send her back to me whenever I might think it necessary, so as to continue the treatment. He hoped that I would, when such circumstances arose, consent to attend her, which he believed I would, knowing my generous nature and my fatherly affection for the girl. She was, he said, fortunate in that she had not only her natural father, but through her affliction had acquired another.

All this was so gracefully phrased that I believed him in all good faith and, despite her misgivings, returned his daughter to him on the eighth of June. On the ninth—the very next day—I was astonished to hear that her family asserted that she was still blind and subject to fits. I felt that this must be some malevolent rumor. But word soon confirmed this outrageous falsehood. The dreadful parents invited people to their home and, showing the girl, compelled her to imitate fits and blindness. This was contradicted by persons who were convinced of the contrary, including several who were unknown to me but who had visited the girl at my house. Once again the poor girl was pulled between opposing poles of truth and falsehood, agitating her fluids to the point where the parents' falsehood would become a

*perverse truth—and her sight vanish irrev-
ocably into interior darkness. While I had little
respect for Paradies, it was clear to me that
he was a tool of several intriguers who did not
wish me or my methods well. Some came
forward—persons completely unknown to me
—and testified that the girl was blind. Behind
them, I was convinced, hid the real source of
my persecution, my medical colleagues discomforted by my successes. Their influence at
court far exceeded my own.*

*In this predicament, I marshaled the testi-
mony of my friends to the best of my ability
—M. de Spielman, Aulic Councilor to Their
Majesties and Director of the State Chancel-
lory; Their Majesties' Councilors, MM. de
Molitor and d'Umlauer, physician to Their
Majesties; de Boulanger, de Heufeld, Baron
de Colnbach, and M. de Weber, who, independent of several other persons, had almost
every day followed for themselves my processes and results.*

*In spite of my perseverance, I saw a proven
truth redirected, little by little, into an area
of uncertainty and conjecture.*

*You can imagine how I was affected by the
relentlessness of my enemies and by the in-*

gratitude of the Paradies family. During the
last half of 1777, though distracted and troubled, I continued my work as best I could. I
turned to other patients, curing one Zwelferine, whose eyes were in a more serious condition than Marie Thérèse's. However, by
December, wearied by the labors of twelve
years and by the continued animosity of my
enemies, I felt that my responsibilities had
been fully discharged and that there was nothing to detain me in Vienna. My research and
treatments had reaped no satisfaction other
than that of which adversity could not de-
prive me.

With the conviction that justice would one
day be done, I decided to travel for the sole
purpose of securing the relaxation I so much
needed. To guard against prejudice and lies,
I arranged for some of my patients, including
the girl Zwelferine, to stay in my home with
my wife and her servants, where their condition could be ascertained at any moment,
thereby certifying the truth of their cures.
They remained eight months after my departure from Vienna and left only on orders from
a higher authority.

My adversaries, who were ever on the watch

*to harm me, lost no time in spreading warnings
about me upon my arrival in Paris.*

. . .

Nothing in this account touched on my uneasi-
ness about possible transgressions of my medical role in treating Marie Thérèse. It did as
much to upset as reassure me. For it was written in that formal mode that was the fashion
of the day, and which now seems somewhat
archaic to me. In it there is the professional
reserve, the distance appropriate to my profession. Between its lines I can still read vivid
life, as recollection supplies details long forgotten. But nowhere, in the lines or between
them, do I find evidence against myself. Nor
do I find convincing evidence by which to par-
don myself. Why this torment should afflict
me, I cannot understand. Stimulated by this
account, these events, forty years later, returned to me a familiar emotion, combining
exasperation, anger, regret, and a sense of
enormous resistance, a wall composed of the
fears and envy of the many who opposed me.
What is it in man that resists the truth, even
when the evidence is placed before his eyes?
My life has been guided by a belief that truth

is a force that makes its own way, by its own virtue. Having watched the truth, and the evidence that supports it, discounted, perverted, ravaged with hatreds and prejudices that answer to men's self-interests, I now must abandon this notion. I have watched while error assumed the face of truth and, so masked, drew to it the approval of those who reject the genuine in favor of a substitute. How does the truth survive at all, either as an idea to which all pay lip service, or as a force that guides many lives which we must honor for their selflessness and for loving truth above themselves? But truth seems to seek out those most powerless to advance its cause, putting them at risk in a world that finds the truth dangerous. To my dying day, which is not far off, I will believe in the truth of those harmonies which regulate the perfection of our lives, those tides of the magnetic sea which I have, in my small way, encouraged to flow through broken bodies and spirits. What was the truth in the case of Marie Thérèse? Distance is supposed to aid the judgment, but I must confess to puzzlement. Her case was obvious: the darkness, as I have often said, was in her mind and not her eyes.

But what is the truth of *my* case? What

shaped the circumstances of my departure from Vienna to Paris where the same angels and devils awaited me in different disguise? There was Paradies's madness, his wife's hysteria, the girl's agonies. That much is beyond argument. But how was Paradies moved, and by whom? How much did the matter of the Empress's pension enter? Was Stoerk commanded by the Empress? Which doctors spoke to him, or to her? Why did my friends' evidence go for nothing when many of them were not without influence? Did they represent themselves to others as they did to me? Were there alliances and conspiracies of which I am still unaware?

At times I can see how each link makes a logical chain leading to my departure from Vienna. More often, things whirl about so that the logic of the events dissolves into a cloud where I cannot see my hand in front of my face. There are times when events so predispose themselves that I seem on the verge of understanding everything. The next day, this hypothesis is destroyed by an overlooked fact, or a new speculation about how things were. I have been giving too much time to this when my thoughts should be otherwise engaged. But reflection at this distance haunts me with the possibility of a truth that will put my mind to rest on something that now disturbs it unduly. There are times when I see all the actors, myself included, as in a play, and they are all strange to me. I see my own face with a lack of emotion that makes me uneasy, for I seem to have trespassed into someone else's thoughts, and some courteous part of me half-apologizes for this transgression. Then, truly, I am not myself.

This strangeness is not new to me. At times in all our lives the familiar seems quite unknown to us, as if what we are looking at had been replaced by a replica, accurate to the last detail but bereft of all familiarity. This was brought home to me last week when I returned from the lake. The experience remains in my mind as an island of strangeness.

I had taken my usual walk to the lake, studied as usual the light on its surface which this day was so rippled as to shatter the sun into a shower of pinpoints, a sight that always gives me a feeling of exaltation. On the way back, without noticing it until I noticed it, if that makes sense, the familiar landmarks became strange to me. I saw the blasted tree—hit by lightning last year—but its dead branches against the sky looked as if seen in a stereopticon, and my hand, when I stretched it in front of me, was miniaturized as if it were a long way away. The stone wall bordering the road to my left, as I proceeded, became entirely unfamiliar, the patterns in the stones redisposing themselves so as to convince me that I had never seen them before. I saluted Herr Wychin and his Frau, but they were so foreign to me that I noticed how the features of his face did not go together, and that the way his wife rocked from side to side as she walked, when I stopped and looked after them, was entirely new to my perceptions.

None of this frightened me. Instead it produced a kind of calm, as when we see something reversed in a mirror and know it to be the same but with a different aspect. As I approached my house, which was around the next bend, my neighbor's dog ran out, as was his habit, to greet me. He had no difficulty in recognizing me, nor I him, despite the fact that he looked exactly like a substitute for himself to the last detail. Indeed, I had never noticed before how plain he was, with his quivering jowls and short, stout legs. My hand proffered its usual greeting, which he accepted, even though I had a notion that it—the hand—did not belong to me. When I turned the bend of the road, my house was exactly as I anticipated, but again, I felt I had never seen it before—its high roof was too tall for the rest of it, and I had a fancy that the house was looking at me through its windows and finding me equally strange.

I entered and sat down by the window, and eventually mute and wordless things resumed their familiar voices, speaking to me as they had always done of common and shared experiences. I found it remarkable that though all was strange (though exactly the same), I had no difficulty in recognizing the tree or dog or house. I knew they were the same but had disguised themselves through some alchemy of exact replication. This strangeness has not revisited me again. Was my body giving notice that it was no longer at home in the world of familiar things, that it would soon take leave of my spirit?

. . .

I dreamed last night that I was attending my own autopsy. I watched from above my body laid on the table, the attending physician bent over it. I myself was also on the opposite side of the table, though I could not see myself clearly. I was thus in a position to look down

on my live and dead selves. As I have frequently said these past months, I am convinced that my bladder is diseased and is the
cause of my death. The other physician made
the incision through my naked abdomen, and,
pushing the muscles aside in an excellent dis-
section, exposed my bladder. He made notes
on its external appearance in a notebook to his
side on a small table, and then cut into the
bladder and everted it. This exposed to my
sight a growth in the wall of the bladder in the
trigonal area, invading the walls and consid-
erable in size. I spoke through my live self
from across the table while I watched from
above and, with satisfaction, indicated the cor-
rectness of my diagnosis. To my irritation, the
other physician, faceless but with spectacles,
professed to see no indication of disease in the
bladder and despite my admonition was about
to extend his inquiry by cutting into the
thorax, which made me extremely uncomfortable, for I have never had trouble with my
lungs or heart. My irritation was such that I
woke up and the first light over the lake fully
recalled me to a waking state.

This dream has left me in no doubt that my
final journey is at hand. The gypsy's prophecy
will come to pass without resistance. As the

sky lightens, I start the business of composing myself to enter the infinite magnetic sea. The other physician's reluctance to perceive the evidence, however, accompanies me with a lingering sense of dissatisfaction.

This novel is based on an incident in the life of Franz Anton Mesmer. The manuscript that Mesmer discovers in chapter five is freely adapted from Captain V. R. Myers's 1948 translation of Dr. Mesmer's 1779 treatise, *Mémoire sur la découverte du magnétisme animal*. See *Mesmerism*, introduction by Gilbert Frankau (London, 1948).

It is unlikely that Mlle. Paradies encountered Mozart during her treatment with Dr. Mesmer, though they appear to have met earlier. They met again at Salzburg in 1783, and Mozart later wrote a concerto for her (B-flat, K. 456). Mlle. Paradies's teachers included Kozeluch and Salieri, both of whom influenced her compositions. She made a European reputation as a concert pianist and singer, often performing her own work, touring such cities as Paris, Prague, Berlin, and London. In 1808 she founded an institute for music education in Vienna. She died in 1824, at the age of sixty-five.

About the Author

Brian O'Doherty is well known in the world of visual arts, about which he has written extensively. He lives in New York with his wife, Barbara Novak.